Sherlock Holmes's
Tibetan Adventure

SHERLOCK HOLMES'S TIBETAN ADVENTURE

John F. Rice

ROBERT HALE · LONDON

ISBN 978-0-7090-9111-0

Robert Hale Limited
Clerkenwell House
Clerkenwell Green
London EC1R 0HT

www.halebooks.com

2 4 6 8 10 9 7 5 3 1

Typeset in 11/17pt New Century Schoolbook
Printed and bound in Great Britain by MPG Books Group,
Bodmin and King's Lynn

CHAPTER 1

❦

I am not a man to often experience fear, but cold dread descended on me, like a fall of snow off a roof, as I realized that I was trapped.

On my right rose the rock face over which the Reichenbach Falls poured noisily from the cliff edge high above me, and on my left the waterfall cascaded past me into the abyss below, where it became a raging torrent. The viewing place where I stood was above a precipice, with no hope of escape downwards.

Standing on the path, blocking my way back, was Professor Moriarty. A man at least as tall as I and just as fit. He carried a walking-stick. I had nothing which I could use as a defensive weapon.

'Made your will, Sherlock Holmes?'

'Where's Doctor Watson?' I asked.

'That buffoon. He's back at your hostelry by now.'

'May I write him a message, before...?'

'Get on with it man.'

I wrote a note which I hoped Watson would find and pinned it beneath my silver cigarette case which I left on a boulder.

'Now get on with it.' I pointedly looked at Moriarty's walking-stick, which I knew disguised a high-powered air rifle capable of killing a man. At least my death would be quick.

For answer Moriarty threw the weapon to the ground. 'I shall strangle you slowly with my bare hands. You have irretrievably disrupted my criminal organization,' he snarled as he walked towards me. 'I will succeed where my hired assassins have failed.' He lurched forward.

I pushed the heel of my walking-boot into the mud and crouched down just in time as he hurled his full weight at me, hands outstretched before him clawing at my neck. My knowledge of the Japanese art of baritsu wrestling made me sway my body instinctively, allowing me to fling both arms around Moriarty's chest. My next move should have been to slip my arms beneath his armpits and lock both hands at the back of my opponent's neck. Moriarty was too quick for me. He twisted his body forward and towards the cliff face, kicking his booted foot backwards and hitting me on the shin. My sturdy boot saved me and my reaction was swift indeed. I caught Moriarty a blow with the side of my hand across his neck. The blow was aimed at his carotid. As was intended, Moriarty seemed stupefied – for a moment only – but it was all that I needed to give him the fatal push.

With flailing arms Moriarty plunged screaming into the maelstrom below. I stood panting to recover my breath and looked to see whether Moriarty's body would rise in the whirlpool or be carried down river. I never saw him again, but I was left with the combined and everlasting vision of a horizontal rainbow at the base of the cataract, sparkling with spray in a shaft of sunlight.

I would have made the ultimate sacrifice in order to rid the planet of such an evil man but fate had decreed that it was not to be necessary. That fate should treat me so favourably struck me as being to some purpose. But what purpose? That thought, coupled with the instinct that even now my life was still in danger from one or more of Moriarty's confederates, led me to look around for a suitable place of concealment.

Picking up Moriarty's walking-stick on my way I decided to climb the rock, and I searched for a possible place to hide.

With difficulty I climbed part way up the cliff overlooking the falls until I was able to take refuge upon a ledge several feet wide and covered with soft moss. It was there that I determined to allow the world to think that Sherlock Holmes too had perished with Professor Moriarty. I decided to lie there until dusk.

I do not consider myself to be an emotional man but I confess that my resolve almost weakened when, later, I heard the sounds of a small search party below the mossy ledge and the despairing voice of my good friend Watson calling, 'Holmes, Holmes, for God's sake speak to me! Tell me that you are not dead.' I remained silent. The Reichenbach Falls roared their defiance at my friend.

'Holmes, where are you?' I heard his voice break. 'Oh, Holmes.' And I believe that poor Watson cried.

I thrust my kerchief into my mouth and bit it hard. The words of my namesake Oliver Wendell Holmes came to me then: *Sin has many tools but a lie is a handle that fits them all.* And I thought about my decision and I was ashamed that by keeping silent I was telling my closest friend such a terrible and distressing lie.

Once more I heard Watson call out, 'You and I, Holmes, will meet again on the sunny shores of eternity – that place of the ultimate mystery.' And I beat the moss flat beneath my fists in frustration, for there was now no turning back. I dared not alter my position lest he or any members of the party with him should perceive me if they looked back on their return to Meiringen.

I had intended to lie low until dusk but sometime later a huge rock, falling from above, boomed past me, struck the path, and bounded over into the abyss. For an instant only, I thought it was a natural occurrence, but I flashed my gaze up and saw a man's head silhouetted against the darkening sky, and another stone struck the very ledge upon which I lay, within a foot of my head. It was obvious that one of Moriarty's confederates had been a witness to all that had taken place and even now was endeavouring to deprive me of my life.

Abandoning Moriarty's walking-stick, and without a second thought, I lowered myself from the ledge and down the cliff side just as another stone sang past me. Terror gave my fingers the grip of metalworkers' vices and my feet wings as I descended. Even so, about ten feet from the path I misjudged my footing and fell but, by the grace of God, I landed, torn and bloody, safely upon the path.

I took to my heels and headed south-east, doing ten miles through the Alps aided only by faint moonlight. My enemy should expect me to head for France, where I have relatives, and so I headed for Florence, where I arrived a week later. It was on the platform at Florence railway station, which I shall always hold in my heart with affection, that I knew my life was about to change.

I was able to telegraph my brother Mycroft that I needed to 'vanish' from the civilized world for twelve months. Mycroft is a very high-ranking civil servant and would be able to furnish me with money and a new identity.

I dared not telegraph Watson for fear of endangering his life and that of Mrs Hudson.

I just hoped that Inspector Patterson had in his possession the blue envelope I had furnished him with, and containing the papers he needed to provide the proof to convict the members of Moriarty's gang already in his custody.

I was convinced that the head I saw silhouetted as I lay on that ledge was none other than that of Colonel Moran, Moriarty's second-in-command, and a marksman who would use every endeavour to destroy me. I was glad that I had picked up Moriarty's powerful air-gun. Moran would surely have picked me off and killed me where I lay on that mossy ledge if I had left the gun where Moriarty abandoned it.

What I in fact received from Mycroft was a Norwegian passport, of all nationalities, in the name of Thor Sigerson, and with a British Empire visa.

The accompanying note from Mycroft recommended that I use the alias of Sigerson to avoid my enemies, and to release press reports from time to time in that name so that he would know that I was alive and well. He enclosed a Norwegian phrase book which I glanced through. The language appeared to consist mainly of long words which I would have difficulty in pronouncing, so I threw the phrase book away.

Naturally, Mycroft had made financial arrangements, but

I was more interested in a letter of introduction which also accompanied his note. The letter was addressed to Mr Jack Blackburn at the offices of the Indian Civil Service in Calcutta and was sealed.

I remember feeling my pulse quicken. For what purpose was this letter intended? And what were the explorations which Herr Thor Sigerson was intended to undertake?

I sat and lit my pipe and gave the matter my consideration. Mycroft could just as easily have furnished me with a British passport in the name of John Smith, but admittedly I would then be easier to trace.

Looking again at the visa allowing Sigerson access into any part of the British Empire, and at his profession of explorer, I wondered: just where did Mycroft expect his brother to explore? I quickly reasoned that as Sigerson was Norwegian, and therefore used to mountainous terrain and a cold climate, that it would be that type of territory which I would be expected to challenge.

First I must introduce myself to Blackburn in Calcutta, but to what purpose I was unable to fathom. Perhaps he was to render assistance to me in my explorations? When I met Blackburn I would ask him why my brother considered it so important that I should make his acquaintance. I had to give up guessing why. In any case, it was best that I should disappear so that, it must be hoped, Colonel Moran would think that I had perished from exposure in my flight from him. Calcutta was as good a place as any to disappear.

I purchased clothing, toiletries and a silver cigarette case to replace the one that I had left on a boulder at Reichenbach together with a note addressed to Watson anticipating my death.

I travelled to Leghorn and embarked on a ship carrying textiles to Djibouti via the Suez Canal route. From Djibouti I voyaged on another ship bound for Bombay and disembarked there on the fifteenth day of June. It was now one month since my fight with Moriarty and I could still hear his horrible scream in my head as he plunged to his death.

Watson had told me of the Indian railway system when relating to me his adventures in that country and in Afghanistan. It was all the experience he had described – and more!

I was impressed by the palatial buildings and appalled at the poverty of India. We did not stop anywhere without the train being besieged by beggars, and when I dined at a rail-side table and left any remains of my meal on the plate there was always a small child lurking somewhere nearby to steal the scraps before they could be properly cleared away. And the smell of India! Spices, incense and the Great Stink of London before Sir Joseph Bazalgette laid down the sewerage system.

I was tempted to write to Watson but, mindful of my dear friend's affection for me, I feared that he might utter some innocent indiscretion which would betray my secret.

I was glad to arrive at Calcutta, where I rested in the coolest recesses of the Great Eastern Hotel to recover from my travels. I had been under severe strain for these past four months and was pleased to discover the restoration of my strength.

Fortunately by now my reputation was well established both in Britain and in Europe. My financial security was ensured by rewards received from the reigning family of Holland, the Coburg branch of the City & Suburban Bank, and from the King of Bohemia. I could afford to remain away from Baker Street for a long time if by so doing I could ensure everyone's safety.

CHAPTER 2

⌘

Early in July I presented myself with my letter of introduction to Mr Blackburn. He was a tall and slender man and neatly dressed. He had a short round face and deep-blue sparkling eyes. His fair curly hair receded from his high, round forehead. He received me with some diffidence.

'Please take a seat, Herr Sigerson.'

His office was spacious, light and airy, and made comfortable by the movement of air provided by a large square woven raffia fan operated by an unseen punkah wallah.

Blackburn opened the envelope from Mycroft using an ivory paperknife. He read the letter. He pursed his lips.

'You obviously have no idea of the contents of your brother's letter,' he stated, 'so if you will accept an invitation to dine with me this evening, I shall prepare a little experiment which should startle you.'

'How gracious of you,' I replied, 'and, of course, I accept.'

At this point Blackburn took up the ivory paperknife and, holding it between finger and thumb, offered it to me vertically.

'Quite an intricate carving, don't you think, sir?' He thrust the paperknife in my direction for me to take it. I was obliged to take it from him by the blade using my forefinger and thumb. 'Local craftsmanship,' he added.

If it had been other than a mere paperknife I would have considered it most discourteous to have had a knife offered to me to take by any other part than the handle. I had no sooner remarked on the native delicate craftsmanship than he took the paperknife back by the handle and replaced it carefully on his desk.

'Eight o'clock shall we say, then?'

'Certainly,' I replied.

Blackburn quickly wrote out an address for me. 'I look forward to entertaining you, sir.' He said it with warm amusement crinkling the skin at the corners of his eyes.

I was puzzled about the business of the paperknife. I assumed that Blackburn had addressed me as 'sir' rather than using my real name because of the possibility of someone, such as the punkah wallah perhaps, on the other side of the office wall, overhearing my true identity.

That evening I travelled in a gharry from the Great Eastern Hotel to a suburb of single-storey houses. The driver was accompanied by a white dog which sat beside him. During the daytime anything up to fifty per cent of the population of Calcutta crowd the thoroughfares. Even now the driver had to exercise care to avoid running in to people gossiping on the street.

On our second meeting Blackburn greeted me warmly at the door of his residence, then lowered his voice.

'Forgive me for addressing you as Herr Sigerson,' he glanced at a servant, 'but your brother has given me good reasons to do so. It is better that you are presumed dead as per the reports in the press.' He stared over my shoulder.

I turned to see what interested him and watched the gharry being driven out of the drive. I must have frowned.

'Some people are ever on the lookout to supplement their income. Even here, a name, unguardedly spoken, could result in payment from the right recipient. Especially when a man has an extra mouth to feed.'

Blackburn led the way to the veranda. I had a vague idea that Colonel Sebastian Moran had been posted in Bengal during his army career and so recognized the merit of Blackburn's caution.

'You mean the dog?' I queried. I must admit that I had noticed cattle, holy to Hindus, and the occasional stray dog scavenging in the streets, none of them with any obvious owner. Personally, I was more interested in the snake-charmer's cobras, performing monkeys, and little boys wearing only a loin-cloth but producing objects seemingly out of thin air. 'If he can't afford to feed it then why not dispose of it?'

'Because he probably cannot,' replied Blackburn, 'by reason that it is possibly regarded as a reincarnation of a close relative: parent, son or daughter, brother or sister, or cousin-brother.' He shrugged. 'Families are very close-knit and a male cousin is regarded equal to a brother.'

We partook of a whisky each and I smoked a cigarette.

'Perhaps the relative lived a somewhat profligate life and karma decreed that he or she returned as a dog as punishment. It is often difficult for Westerners to understand the Eastern mind in these matters.'

We sat and talked until the cerulean sky gave way to a velvet blue followed suddenly by star-filled black. We dined on a mild chicken curry, boiled rice and vegetables, accompanied by mango chutney. I noted that Blackburn ate heartily and received the impression that he enjoyed the most robust health and enthusiasm for life.

After we finished our meal we sat for about an hour discussing London, the Empire, the Germans, the Irish question, and the latest skirmish which was always taking place with the Chinese, since the Opium Wars. Blackburn looked at me oddly throughout the rest of these discussions, but, before I could question him, he said, 'I promised to show you an experiment.'

'You promised to startle me,' I reminded him. 'I doubt very much you will do that. Certainly not now that I'm forewarned.'

'You think not? We shall see.' Blackburn led me to his study. Once there he took a sealed envelope out of his desk drawer and handed it to me. 'Kindly place this in your pocket but please initial it first.'

'What is this?' I enquired. 'A conjuring trick?'

'No legerdemain this, but proof. Something which in years to come will contribute to your skills. Now put it into your pocket, please.'

I did as he bade.

Blackburn poured water from a jug into a handbasin. 'Will you please wash your hands for me?' He handed me a towel and placed a soap container beside the basin.

I carried out his request. Meanwhile, he had been preparing something on his desk.

'May I ask you to place the thumb and forefinger of your right hand on to this pad, please?' Blackburn took my right hand and placed my finger squarely on to the pad, rocked my hand a little and did the same with my thumb. He raised my hand to inspect the results and, satisfied, said, 'Now place your finger on to this sheet of paper. That's it.' He rocked my finger gently. When he removed my finger from the sheet of paper I saw a perfect ridge-print in black with white furrows on its surface. Blackburn repeated the process with my right thumb. He emitted an 'Ah,' of satisfaction. 'Now if you would wash the black off, please.'

Blackburn stood a little apart from me while I washed and dried my hands. 'Please sit at my desk.'

I sat, my thumb and forefinger ridge-prints before me on the sheet of paper.

'Now open the envelope and take out the contents.'

I noted the eagerness on Blackburn's face as I opened the envelope and spread a single sheet of paper taken from it beside the one bearing my prints. On the paper was drawn with great accuracy a representation of the ridges of a thumb and finger.

'Please compare them with your own.' He handed me a magnifying lens and pushed the oil lamp closer.

The two ridge-prints drawn were exactly the same as those Blackburn had just printed from my thumb and forefinger. I could not help but draw in my breath sharply and I immediately checked my initials on the envelope.

'Have I not startled you?'

'Yes,' I admitted, 'but how…?'

For answer Blackburn produced the ivory paperknife I had handled that very morning at his office. On one side were the black ridges of my near perfect thumb ridge-print. Blackburn turned the knife over to reveal my fingerprint on the other side. I admit, I sat and stared at him. Its possibilities did not elude me.

'If,' said Blackburn slowly, 'that had been a real knife found protruding from a dead person and your ridge-prints had been found on the handle, you would assuredly go to the gallows, Mr Holmes.'

Before the full implication had been absorbed by my stunned brain, he continued, 'Everyone has different finger and thumb ridge-prints. Everyone. They are our individual identity marks. They do not vary from the cradle to the grave save from accidental scarring. I am surprised that you appear not to have even heard of it!'

'I must admit that it is a branch of detection which I have neglected.' I cursed myself inwardly. Had not Mycroft once discussed Purkinje's work on finger-ridges! Work which was undertaken earlier this century. The vases of Japanese potters had been identified by their impressed finger-ridges on the base.

'You did not read the letters submitted to the British Scientific Journal *Nature* by Henry Faulds and William Herschel?'

I had to confess they had escaped my attention.

'Sir William served in the Indian Civil Service as a magistrate in Hooghly until '78 when he returned to England. However, during his service as a magistrate, he was concerned with cases of attempted fraud by impersonation, where the rightful recipient of a Government pension had died. Sir William first of all had hand prints taken to verify the identity of the true recipient. Subsequently, he found that finger-ridge prints were quite adequate to prevent further fraud. I use his system on important documents in my department to this day.'

I shook my head. It must have been some ten years ago. I

thought back. Then I remembered. 'Very remiss of me and, as it is evidenced, a grave omission on my part. I was heavily committed that year to solving quite a number of cases, several of which have never been offered for publication, and two which were most interesting. My colleague, Doctor John Watson, has recorded the two under the titles of *The Valley of Fear* and *The Sign of Four*. I hope that you may be interested to read them when publication makes them freely available. I neglected to renew my subscription to *Nature* that year because of pressure of investigations. Has your system been used to any effect?'

'Oh yes, to very good effect. Certain items were taken from the office of the Indian Civil Service and the culprit was apprehended and charged on the strength of his ridge-prints. A senior man. He confessed. All very distressing. Who knows, perhaps you or Scotland Yard may use this system one day?'

Blackburn was good enough to divulge to me his discoveries using lamp-black or powdered chalk to dust items with a smooth or polished surface to reveal ridge-prints, and his use of a mixture of lamp-black and oil on a wad of calico to transfer prints from a suspect's fingers on to paper. We compared our own finger-ridges with others that Blackburn had collected. He has classified them basically as Plain Arch, Tented Arch, Loop, Double Loop, Whorl and Accidental, but it was evident that some better system of classification would have to be devised before Scotland Yard or anybody could make effective use of finger-ridge printing in the detection of crime.

'And now to the subject of Tibet.'

'Tibet!' I exclaimed. This was even more startling than the

finger-ridge experiment. Then light dawned. 'Of course! Tibet. The nearest mountainous terrain to Calcutta must assuredly be Himalaya and then Tibet!'

'Correct.'

'What a fool I've been!' I remember slapping my forehead.

It was Blackburn's turn to be startled. 'I don't understand.'

'I'll explain. My parents were both killed in a train accident twenty years ago. It was at their burial. I remember as I turned from their grave in Crowborough that I pleaded with my brother, 'Why? Why did they have to die?'

'Understandable,' said Blackburn.

'Mycroft shrugged his shoulders and said to me, "I just do not know. It is God's will."

"What is the meaning, if any, of life and death?" I asked him, "and is there life after death?" Mycroft put his arm around my shoulders and understood my suffering.' I began to feel embarrassment. 'I was seventeen, Mr Blackburn. Young. Inexperienced. It was the year before I started at Oxford, where I quickly matured.'

'Death is bewildering to us all, Mr Holmes. But you were going to say something about Tibet?'

'My brother said, "You might be better consulting a spiritual person such as the Dalai Lama of Tibet rather than me. He, of all people, might know the answer to the ultimate mystery." '

Are there not subtle forces at work of which we know little? Had it not been a strange thing for Watson to cry out, 'You and I, Holmes, will meet again on the sunny shores of eternity – that place of the ultimate mystery.'

Evidently, Mycroft had never forgotten my plea and had discreetly suggested by association that this was the opportunity to combine my feigned death with a visit to the Dalai Lama. Mycroft knew that I had not forgotten what he said on that fateful day, and, he knew about the secret deathbed experiments at Bart's. He was one of very few people privy to Sir James Saunders's and my experiments into our search for the soul.

Blackburn seemed abashed at my revelation. 'But why the Dalai Lama? Why not the vicar who took the service?'

'You must understand, Mr Blackburn, that my brother was but twenty-four at the time and poised on the threshold of what has proved to be a brilliant career. He too was vastly upset and it was probably the first thing that came into his head in his shocked state of mind.'

'I still do not understand, Mr Holmes. Why go to Tibet when you could have visited the Vatican when you were in Italy?' He stopped short as though struck by an idea.

I waited but he did not reveal the thought to me. I too found the notion rather curious. Why Tibet indeed? My brother is a high-ranking Civil Servant advising the Government. Sometimes, with the influence – nay power – he seems to wield, I think he is the Government! Perhaps he has another reason or purpose in my visiting the Dalai Lama? 'I do not understand either, Mr Blackburn, but I have a feeling that destiny is drawing me to that mysterious country!'

'Well, Mr Holmes, Tibet is forbidden to foreigners. Tibetans do not welcome strangers. You will have considerable difficulty in gaining entry. You will need specialized assistance. And even then, if you were to reach Lhasa it is extremely doubtful that you will be allowed to remain. Your best chance is to arrive in Lhasa just as the winter snows seal off Tibet from the outside world. The authorities will then have to allow you to stay until the spring thaw.'

I recognized the merit of Blackburn's suggestions.

'Timing is of the essence,' continued Blackburn. 'You will need to enter Tibet during September and you will probably arrive in Lhasa some six to eight weeks later. By November the snows will have closed all of the mountain passes. I suggest that you travel by rail to Darjeeling where I will contact you with as much information and assistance as I can muster. And the best of luck to Herr Sigerson!'

Before I left Calcutta I posted a paragraph to *The Times* in the name of Thor Sigerson so that Mycroft would be reassured of my progress.

I took what is called the Toy Train from Calcutta, a journey from which I am sure I will retain everlasting memory of its holy men, called Saddhus, on the banks of the Hooghly, and of its dreadfully impoverished lower-caste citizens.

It was not until the train was passing fields of opium poppies as it travelled northwards through Bengal that I remembered that enigmatic look on Blackburn's face. The Opium Wars. The Government was afraid of the Chinese, the Yellow Peril as it was called, entering our jewel of the Empire, India, to take over that lucrative trade. But then I completely dismissed the notion that opium could have anything to do with my brother's letter and my intended visit to Tibet.

CHAPTER 3

✐

As the Toy Train wound its way around the Batasia loop
on the last part of my journey to Darjeeling I had an
attack of vertigo. The scenery was magnificent with dense
greenery below rocky precipices but I was unable to enjoy it.
As a diversion, I took stock of my assets.

Apart from the clothing, toiletries and travel bags I had
purchased en route, I had my pipe and tobacco pouch, ciga-
rettes in a new silver case, matches also in a silver vesta
case, my lens, pocket watch, pocket knife and my ear-flapped
travelling cap. I compiled a list in my pocket notebook of
what I considered an explorer would require to facilitate his
profession. I found the exercise extremely therapeutic.

I listed a change of stout boots and warm clothing, a
supply of notebooks and pencils, a sketch pad for making
maps and diagrams, and a supply of toiletries to last me
twelve months. I recognized that I would need guidance on
what I would really need and this troubled me not a little.

I vaguely wondered whether an explorer should have a
firearm but I decided that I would prefer to rely on a stout
walking-stick. I added that to my list. I also resolved to
supply myself with a hip flask and brandy. I am sure my

friend Watson with his pawky sense of humour would have commented, 'For emergency medicinal purposes only, of course!' I also added a note that I would require pigment to stain my skin brown. I might need to disguise myself.

The train made its precarious way into the valley over which Darjeeling presides and is surrounded by its tea plantations in the foothills. I was glad to alight and enjoy the comforts of the Victoria Hotel and to have escaped the oppressive summer heat of Calcutta.

I was surprised at how cool it was in Darjeeling and how lethargic I felt for several days.

On the third day I received a letter from Blackburn. He wished Herr Sigerson fortune in his explorations and was pleased to advise that Her Majesty's Government had made arrangements to facilitate his explorations of the British Empire. And that was all. No information, no contacts, no advice, no suggestions. I really had no alternative but to fume at this seeming impasse and endeavour to be patient and wait for something to happen.

With an unknown period of time on my hands I set out to explore Darjeeling. It was a town set on a sock-shaped hill. The town was tiered and was a maze of steps and terraces. Everywhere seemed to be a long way down or an even longer way up. It was inhabited by a diversity of peoples of many cultures and complexions.

My hotel room afforded me an uninterrupted view of Kanchenjunga, but wherever I looked around Darjeeling there were snow-capped mountains. Around the bases of the mountains were dense forests.

I visited several tea gardens and also Lloyds Botanical Gardens. I wondered at the many *chortens* – small shrines –

erected by Buddhists. I had been told that *chortens* inspire meditation and the attaining of a mental state of the inner light.

I also visited areas of very English gingerbread-trim cottages and single-storey houses.

I found myself increasingly drawn to an interest in Buddhism, and to the Yiga Cholung monastery at Ghoon on Tiger Hill, which I visited a number of times at different parts of the day. There is a single window in the roof which allows a beam of light to penetrate the gloom. The light illuminates the massive seated image of Maitreya, the Buddha to come, behind the front altar. Around the walls are frescos and around the Messiah Buddha are flags, drums and stacks of prayer stools. The Messianic element common to Judaism, Christianity and Buddhism did not escape me.

Tiger Hill is noted for its views and is the place from which to watch dawn break. I am not by nature an early riser but I was told that the golden glow of the rising sun changes the colour of the snow-capped peaks to crimson, pink and shining gold. Laziness ordains that normally I would be unable to verify such a graphic description. However, I had the most terrible nightmare of Moriarty shooting me with his air-gun, resulting in my falling screaming through a rainbow. I could not get back to sleep and so I visited Tiger Hill for the last time. As I sat and watched the dawn painting the snow-capped mountains I found myself being joined by Buddhist monks in their rust-coloured robes. An overwhelming sense of peace enveloped me and I have never experienced nightmares of Moriarty again.

One day I visited the tomb of Alexander Koros who died on his way to Lhasa in eighteen forty-two, and, as that is my destination, Koros's death had a rather profound significance for me.

I usefully occupied my time in purchasing all the items on my list. I had time to experiment with vegetable dyes and permanganate of potash to colour my skin.

Also, by some good fortune, I was able to purchase an old violin and bow in their case as I browsed in the local bazaar. It helped to amuse me during many empty hours.

During this time I was able to read a picturesque account of my demise in an old copy of *The Times*, written by my old friend Watson. I underlined in the journal that I was by now keeping on a daily basis that I was pleased that I had not endangered his life nor that of Mrs Hudson.

Many days later I had a visitor: a man about five feet in height with dark skin and bright, jet-black, alert eyes. He was dressed in a dark-brown tunic top and riding breeches. He was slightly bow-legged, suggesting a lifetime's familiarity with riding. His shoulders and hat had a light layer of dust on them as though he had travelled far. He removed his hat to reveal black, tousled hair.

'Herr Sigerson?'

'I am he.'

He handed me an envelope sealed with red wax. I noted the J.B. impressed in the seal.

'I presume that your horse is being watered. May I offer you refreshment?'

'Please.'

I led the way on to the veranda, opening the envelope on the way. While the man sipped tea I studied the contents.

The single sheet of paper it contained bore a sketch of my thumb ridges which I was able surreptitiously to check. It bore the simple message:

Travel with Nin Lee Deng to Gangtok and he will make all arrangements. He will act as your guide and protector. Trust him implicitly. He knows your brother and has heard of you by reputation but has not been told your real identity. That is for you to reveal when and if you consider it to be prudent. Good Luck.

It was unsigned.

'You come highly recommended, Deng,' I remarked.

He grunted his satisfaction. 'You have stout clothing suitable for riding?'

I nodded my assent.

Within the hour I had settled my bill and Deng had supplied me with two lean and wiry mounts – one to ride and the other to act as packhorse.

Deng was taciturn but on our journey to Gangtok I did elicit that he was fluent enough in English, Nepalese, Hindustani and Tibetan. I had reason to believe that he was fluent in at least one other language.

I had observed that he had a dragon tattooed on the inside of his left wrist. I was certain that it indicated membership of a Chinese Tong.

Deng carried a kukri at his belt.

He settled us in lodgings in Gangtok while he went out to make arrangements for our journey. I was left to explore the town.

In the bazaar I watched craftsmen as they tooled leather,

planishing unidentifiable metals, as well as silver and copper, engraving brassware, chasing and repoussé-embossing silver, carving ivory and wood, and weaving rugs. These craftsmen patterned their wares with intricate interwoven geometrical designs. Even the stocks of ancient muskets offered for sale had been improved by inlaying with attention-compelling motifs. I understood how it came naturally to them to decorate every utensil and artefact. They were inspired by so much beauty surrounding them and framed in the north by the silver-sheened blue of the Himalaya mountains.

Beyond the mountain range lay mysterious Tibet.

CHAPTER 4

U ndoubtedly Deng must have appealed to my sense of vanity.

'You are natural rider. There is little anyone could teach you but...!' We've all had experience of such phrases.

However, Deng had taken us to an area of meadowland and I was soon riding with stirrups crossed across the saddle and folded arms! First my mount walked, and then Deng encouraged it to trot, then it cantered, then it jumped a low bush, and then I fell off.

Because of Deng's encouragement I soon gained in confidence and, like most other seemingly impossible challenges, it soon became easy, almost automatic with practice, to take jumps about three feet high. I understood that it would be prudent to learn how to lead a packhorse and control it in an adverse situation whilst keeping the other hand free for other purposes. I suppose I knew from then on that I would have to carry a firearm and be able to use it while on the move. Why else should it be necessary to ride without recourse to use of the reins?

The day came when Deng advised me that all arrangements had been made. 'Today you meet sirdar, caravan leader, Wangdula. Tonight we sleep under canvas. Tomorrow start for Tibet.' Deng proceeded to give me a *tchomba*, the large Tibetan cloak to wrap around me when we reached the snowline at, I would hazard a guess, about 14,000 feet. He also gave me a *ponkhai*, the traditional Tibetan blanket, to wrap myself in when sleeping, several *khatas* – white muslin scarves which Tibetans exchange on meeting and are equivalent to Western hand-shakes; and last but very important, a Tibetan tea bowl with a cover and saucer all made of polished wood. This, Deng insisted, I would have to become accustomed to carrying on my person at all times. Tibetans, he advised me, always drank from their own tea bowl and there was a strict etiquette surrounding their use.

When I was packing my possessions Deng helped me by putting aside all but my notebook journal and sundry other items, to make the packing as compact as possible. I had to positively insist on including my violin. When I started to remind Deng that we had not purchased comestibles he advised me that it had already been taken care of. He left me muttering, 'Westerners, eat too much and carry too many things with them when they travel.'

My last task was to write a report on the progress of Herr Sigerson in his explorations of Sikkim, and that he intended continuing his explorations in a north-easterly direction from Gangtok – meaning Tibet, of course. I posted it to *The Times*. I imagined that Mycroft would be well satisfied that his ruse had succeeded when he read the article.

We rode some little distance out of Gangtok, perhaps thirty minutes' ride, to an area of rough grazing. Spread around a group of tents were horses, yaks and dzos. Geese honked warning of our approach. I had wondered where Deng had been for hours on end over the past few days.

We tethered our mounts and packhorses to pegs in the ground. Six men gathered around. Deng exchanged *khatas* with the leader and introduced Herr Sigerson to the stocky and muscular-necked man. I exchanged *khatas* with him. This was Wangdula and I judged him to be in his early thirties. In turn I was introduced to the remaining five, with whom I also exchanged *khatas*. We then sat surrounded by the orderly arrangement of tents, many leather-bound bales, large bundles of firewood, baskets, and a group of muskets propped in neat-tented military style.

We drank tea laced with a rancid type of butter and salt. I used my tea bowl for the first time. Wangdula used bowl, lid and saucer. The rest of us used only our tea bowl and saucer.

Wangdula seemed to be the only one with a sufficient knowledge of English for me to be able to converse.

I had ridden into their camp without recourse to using reins; this appeared to have overcome some doubt which Wangdula had previously held. However, I was wearing my ear-flapped travelling cap and Deng explained that Wangdula considered it would be too conspicuous on our travels. A leather cap was found which fitted my head but did not, in my opinion, suit me. It was flat on top and had ear-flaps but was of the style traditional to Tibet. I resolved to wipe the interior with a solution of permanganate of potash to disinfect it before wearing it.

My clothing was suitable for travelling but was not Tibetan. I was offered Tibetan clothing but it was too small for me. I would have to conceal my Western clothing beneath my *tchomba*. It was then agreed to leave the provision of indigenous apparel until an appropriate time and opportunity arose. I would need to find a tailor.

We then settled financial arrangements, after which, Deng and I pitched our tents.

Bonjl was the cook for the group of traders. He spit-roasted two chickens and boiled some vegetables for our evening meal.

I was woken at dawn and breakfasted on a bowl of boiled rice. The beasts were then burdened. Our packhorses carried each man's tent, personal items, *ponkhai*, and a small quantity of provisions: rice, dried beans and suchlike. The dzos, that curious cross between the domestic cow and the yak, carried the bales, packages and panniers, baskets of live geese and fowl, and one basket of pigeons. Only the yaks carried the largest bundles. Yaks were very powerful beasts of burden. Each had a ring through its nose and a shaggy black coat which hung to the ground. Their spread of horns was shortened and the ends rounded off for the safety of the drovers. Four men loaded each double bundle on to them – one on either side to balance them.

I enquired of Wangdula what was in the bundles; he replied that they contained ex-army tents.

I mentioned to Deng the effort it took to load the yaks. 'Surely mere ex-army tents do not weigh that heavily?'

Deng smiled enigmatically but did not reply. Instead he nodded to Wangdula to set the caravan of over eighty animals moving.

Deng's silence had confirmed to me that the yaks were, in all probability, carrying ex-army something. My intuition told me weapons and ammunition. I knew it wouldn't be opium, but just what had Mycroft involved me in?

CHAPTER 5

⟨ornament⟩

We followed an ever narrowing tributary of the River Trista through pine-forested slopes interspersed with groves of rhododendrons, their trunks like those of trees and towering some fifty feet above us.

We spread ourselves along the line of animals carrying their eccentric loads consisting of the goods that I did know about. This caravan carried firewood, aromatic woods, spices, salt, sugar, crystallized fruits in blue-and-white pottery jars, bags of bright dyes for colouring sand from which Tibetan monks create meditative pictures called mandalas, nuts, curios, brassware and fodder. Most of the merchandise was regarded as luxuries in Tibet, and sold well at festival times, so I was informed by Deng.

Gradually we left the forest behind us as we headed for Kampa-dzong. I frequently smoked my pipe to cover the combined smell of animal sweat and dung.

I studied my companions as we took a midday rest, as well as when we were in the saddle. Bonjl had a broad continually smiling face. When he walked he had a rolling gait which I had seen many times in London and which I ascribed to childhood rickets. Despite his quaint walk he was extremely agile. Trethong was taciturn, preferring to exercise his jaws in chewing betel nut rather than talking, and ejecting red sputum at prominent trees and rocks as if to mark the boundaries of his territory.

The early-evening mist hung over the forest now far below us, and veiled the valleys in an enchanting landscape. Around us were high hills and, in the distance, snow-capped mountains. We made camp for the night with one man at a time taking two-hour shifts of sentry duty, aided by the geese in their baskets; they were as alert as any guard-dog. If by chance Colonel Moran had received news of my whereabouts I certainly felt a lot safer.

Two days later and at an altitude of about 8,000 feet we passed by Lachan, the last village of any size in Sikkim. Kanchenjunga loomed some 20,000 feet high to the north-west. We put its blue-and-white icy peak behind us as we turned north-east across the Lonak valley towards the Nago Pass some 18,000 feet above sea level.

From time to time we had to dismount where the terrain was difficult and either had to lead the beasts or pull their nose rings individually, until their reluctance diminished as the going improved.

There was one border post, manned by bored soldiers who waved Wangdula through. Their boredom appeared to be temporarily relieved by a discreetly passed package. I did wonder whether it was opium or some other drug, which I had been openly offered in the several bazaars I had visited and had, with some difficulty, refused.

As we entered the higher slopes I suffered from shortness of breath and shooting pains in my chest. I found it difficult enough to walk and impossible to shout at the beasts and pull at them at the same time, in the more arduous places. I was sitting on a rock gasping, just after having persuaded a dzo to climb up a rocky gully. It was carrying geese and was particularly smelly because of goose-droppings. I was fumbling inside my clothes for my pipe when Deng came by, pulling at another reluctant dzo. 'Give up smoking,' was all he said. It was obvious that my lungs were unable to cope comfortably with the rarified atmosphere. I took his advice and thrust my pipe deep into an inconvenient pocket.

I continued my observation of my companions. Lobsang, despite the hard life that he led, was at heart a religious man; he really should have been a monk. Like many Tibetans who carry a leather or metal talisman called a gaou, Lobsang carried his on his belt and his was the largest I'd seen. It was his habit to control the beasts with a stick held in his right hand while thumbing his rosary of 108 prayer beads in his left hand, marking off his muttered prayers. His serenity had left his face almost devoid of any creases or wrinkles.

Tagstel was lean and wiry and carried pebbles in a bag; this he carried outside his clothing, in contrast to custom. As Tibetan clothing had no pockets, personal items and money were carried in bags suspended from the neck and worn inside the clothing. Tagstel could throw a pebble with considerable accuracy to sting a lagging yak or dzo, to make it catch up with its companions. In recognition of his skill, Tagstel generally brought up the rear. Dzos were smaller than yaks, with tan-and-black coats shorter but no less shaggy than those of the yaks, and horns rounded at the ends to prevent retaliation when the drovers urged them on with pointed goads, sticks and whips.

As we climbed toward the Nago Pass I was glad of my *tchomba* to draw closely around me against the chill of the snow.

It was on this last part of our journey, before we reached Tibet, that Deng informed me that Tibetans abhor the destruction of paper with characters upon it. Under no circumstances was I ever to attempt to burn or even tear paper in the presence of Tibetans. He then went on to say that I should destroy any papers or cards that it would be unwise to have about my person should I be apprehended by the Tibetan border guards or police. I wondered at that point just how much he knew about me, as the whole party referred to me as Sigerson. But my judgement was clouded by the thought of what the yaks might be carrying and so, resenting his advice, I made a pretence of burning papers, excluding my journal, of course. In order to create paper for burning, and, because it seemed eminently sensible, I cut out my name from three visiting cards and placed the narrow strips of card inside my cigarette case, vestas case and my tobacco pouch. I retained my British passport in an inner pocket and Herr Thor Sigerson's in a bag around my neck. The strips of card bearing my name gave me the comforting thought that if, like Koros, I were to die on my way to Lhasa, some diligent searcher would find my real identity and somehow the news would reach Mycroft.

We reached the col, the mountain pass, on the thirtieth day of September and Tibet lay before us. We stopped and stared in awe as the beasts rested and finished the last of the fodder in the sunshine.

Lalam drew up beside me. '*Ya po re*,' he said: Tibetan for 'it is good', or 'it is well'. His eyes glistened with tears at seeing his homeland again.

Clouds drifted below our eye level and Lalam pointed out between them a lake and, beyond, a snow-capped mountain range. He then quoted poetry by Milarespa which I could not understand but which I could see from his inspired expressions were thoughts of great beauty. I remember from my notes that Lalam moved me greatly.

Wangdula observed his homeland through a telescope which he had been carrying. Below us and, as yet, out of sight, were the Dekhogze monastery and the Tibetan border post.

Evidently it was safe to move on because Wangdula gave the signal and we proceeded downwards. The beasts slipped on the icy rock and their stiff, icicled hair sparkled in the sunlight. I tried to take in this strange new world but the glare of the sun off the snow began to distort my vision. Reflex action narrowed my eyelids to mere slits.

Some distance below the snowline we came upon an enormous accumulation of stones and pebbles forming a cone-shaped cairn. All of us added more to 'placate demons' who inhabited this perilous place. Further on and below the snowline we came to another cairn with shredded cloths fluttering on sticks thrust between the stones, indicating what must have once been recognizable prayer banners. We added more stones in gratitude to the deities for keeping us safe.

We pressed on. Wangdula went ahead of us as scout, on the alert for bandits or border guards. We came to a grassy place with a stream and camped there.

Boulders gave us shelter and from between them I was able to observe deep splits in the mountainside. Perhaps they had been formed by a sudden, fearful upheaval caused by an earthquake thousands of years ago. By peering from the top of a boulder I could see the scored mountainside, the high ridges and precipitous cliffs, and below those were slopes which spread in harmonious curves disappearing into the purple haze of distance.

At dusk Wangdula left camp. He returned three hours later with the news that the border post was manned by Men of Kham. These were a tall race of Tibetans whose stature was such that seven feet was quite common. They made up the majority of Tibet's equivalent of our police force.

Under cover of darkness Wangdula had enquired of the monks of Dekhogze as to the occupants of the border post and was relieved to learn that the current garrison was disposed to be lax and friendly. However, they could be certain to wave Wangdula's caravan through without incident in return for some little luxury to alleviate the monotony. What they would not do would be to allow a *phiing* or foreigner to enter Tibet. My height would bring disaster upon us all. I opined that Wangdula was very much afraid that my being discovered would lead to what the yaks were carrying being detected.

At dawn Wangdula and his five companions, Bonjl, Lalam, Trethong, Lobsang and Tagstel, took the caravan and descended into the valley and out of our sight. Meanwhile Deng and I remained concealed in a rocky gully with our horses and packs nearby.

It was now five months since Moriarty had perished in the Falls of Reichenbach, which event had resulted in my presence in Tibet.

Wrapped in our *tchombas*, we listened for the sound of the monastery *ragdongs*, long horn instruments similar to Swiss alpine horns, with which the monks of Tibetan monasteries communicate over vast distances, advising of caravans or strangers in their vicinity. When we heard the sound we knew that Wangdula had arrived at the border post. I imagined him exchanging *khatas* and plying the Men of Kham with gifts before pressing on as quickly as possible, as prudence dictated.

Deng and I slept most of that day. As darkness approached we muffled our horses' hoofs as Wangdula had done on the previous night. We took a most difficult path where the urials, Himalayan wild sheep, roamed and where it would have been impossible to take the yaks and dzos. We proceeded slowly with only the light of a waning moon to help us on our way.

The plan was to meet up with Wangdula near a village called Chorltung in two days' time. It was imperative that I should not be seen by either the border guard or the monks of Dekhogze monastery. If I had been seen, I would assuredly have been escorted back over the Nago Pass.

Dawn oozed gentle colours over the distant mountains and we breakfasted before sleeping again in concealment.

We travelled again during the hours of darkness with the going becoming easier. We joined Wangdula's party just before dawn, setting the geese off honking. Lalam was acting as sentry and greeted us warmly. He made us Tibetan tea with the salty taste and the rancid butter floating on the top and I was glad of it. I was grateful too for the hour or so of sleep before the caravan set off again.

Bonjl killed a goose and we all had a celebratory dinner off it that evening.

Our way dropped through hillsides covered with drifts of maple, pine and rhododendron. The sound of waterfalls splashing into pools came to us from time to time. When I heard those, thoughts of my close encounter with death came back to briefly haunt me.

Baritone voices chanting and the smell of incense carried on the breeze often advised us of the proximity of a monastery before we skirted a cliff or bluff when the sound of *ragdongs* would advise us, as well as the people of the locality, that we had been observed.

Unfortunately, during a rainstorm several days after leaving Chorltung, we came upon a *gompa* – literally 'a dwelling in the solitude'. Our visibility had been obscured and we came upon it quite suddenly.

The inhabitants were a man and a woman. Their curiosity overcame any dislike of the rain, as they came out with *tchombas* over their heads, to see who and what we were.

I dismounted and walked beside my horse, averting my face and stooping, trying to conceal myself. Horror evinced itself in their expressions when they realized that a *philing* was intruding into Tibet. They seemed not to notice Deng, or they did not regard him as a foreigner.

There was much gesticulating and discussion between Wangdula and the couple. Deng did his best to keep me abreast of events but I had already guessed that the couple were insisting that I return to Sikkim the way I had come.

Deng went on to explain that Wangdula had told the couple that I was a magician summoned to assist His Holiness, the Dalai Lama. The man had promptly insisted that I work some magic as proof that I was a magician, or return.

Wangdula shrugged his apology.

By this time the rain had dispersed.

I put my mind to the problem. I am unable to do even a simple party trick. Then a thought struck me. I just had to hope that neither the man nor his wife had ever seen a magnifying lens.

I walked across to the man, stood in front of him and stared at him. He stared insolently back. I then whipped out my lens and held it about two inches in front of my right eye, which was instantly magnified about four times its normal size from where he stood. He stepped back and his jaw dropped. I transferred my lens to a position just in front of my mouth, opened it wide and roared at him like some wild animal. Both he and his wife ran panic-stricken into their *gompa* and slammed the door shut behind them.

Wangdula seemed impressed but with some reservation.

I shrugged. 'I hope I did not overdo the magic.'

Deng and Wangdula looked at each other. Deng said something. Wangdula nodded agreement. Deng turned to me. 'You will be evil demon to them – not magician – unless you give talisman. Good luck symbol.'

I felt helplessly about my person for something resembling a talisman. I took out my new silver cigarette case which had now become obsolete due to the high altitude affecting my lungs. I offered it and raised my eyebrows in query.

Wangdula nodded his head in approval and took it from me. He and Deng hammered on the door of the *gompa* and shouted to the occupants. After a while it was tentatively opened slightly and a hand appeared. Wangdula placed the cigarette case into the hand which was then promptly withdrawn.

At that point I remembered the strip of visiting card

which I had placed inside the case. But I then relaxed in the knowledge that they would be unable to read English anyway.

CHAPTER 6

I think we all gave a sigh of relief that I had been accepted
as a magician and we resumed our journey through the
rugged terrain.

When we rested the animals Wangdula and Deng
unbound the burdens of one of the yaks which did contain an
ex-army tent protecting an inner oilskin-wrapped package.
As I had guessed, it contained firearms. Within it were up to
twenty breech-loading repeating rifles, metallic cartridges,
pistols and their rounds, and a number of grenades.

Deng handed me a revolver and six rounds of ammunition
wrapped in oiled paper. I loaded the revolver chamber with the
six bullets. Deng then searched until he found me a webbing
belt to thrust it into. He then took out rifles for Wangdula,
himself, Tagstel, Trethong and me. Bonjl and Lobsang
preferred their ancient muskets. Wangdula persuaded Lalam
to exchange his ancient firearm for one of the rifles.

The old guns were carefully wrapped in oilsilk and loaded
on to a yak. Deng distributed ammunition belts and thirty
rounds for each rifle, then took out two grenades, which he
placed in his saddlebag. A saddle holster was found for my
rifle and we resumed our journey.

Wherever possible we made detours to avoid close contact with the inhabitants of lamaseries or villages for my safety. The sound of *ragdongs* indicated that we had been sighted and on more than one occasion an inflection of their sonorous tone indicated to Wangdula that there was danger in the area. When this happened one of his party rode to the monastery to ascertain what the danger was; usually it was *tchapas* – bandits, but once it was a landslide. Then he would take advice and change direction to avoid the danger. He then used his telescope even more frequently than usual to keep a constant lookout.

I would have liked to explore the quaint villages with their curled roofs, *chorten*, stone-walled animal pounds, colourful prayer flags and smiling inhabitants.

Such detours to avoid dangers lost us time. If I could have had my way we would have lost even more time. But let that rest!

By now we were travelling on the great plain of Tibet some 10,000 feet above sea level.

Usually outlined against the sky because of their lofty locations we saw mud-brown lamaseries with their confusion of tiled roofs ending in a horn shape, with beribboned poles topped by copper balls and the sails of prayer mills. The sails revolved when the monks manually turned a cogged wheel at their base. On the sails was the mantra '*Om mani padme um*'. The tinkling sound of bronze bells could sometimes be heard. Always, facing the main gate, was the obligatory *chorten*, whitened and pear-shaped.

Occasionally Wangdula, accompanied by Bonjl, would venture into a village to buy or barter fresh vegetables and provisions. On these occasions I would retire into my tent in case a curious villager should visit our camp.

The foothills abounded with wild onion-beds and so from time to time food was redolent with their healthy piquancy.

About once every ten days Deng released a homing pigeon with a cryptic message written on cigarette paper and fastened to a leg. Every time he released one he whispered, 'Beware hawks friend of soldiers.' I understand that he made reference to Herr Sigerson's continued explorations, and, if the pigeon arrived at its destination safely, I assumed the recipient would write up a report suitable as a filler article to be published in *The Times*. I had grave doubts as to the possibility of any of the pigeons completing their homing journey, but I was glad of the reference to Herr Sigerson to keep my brother, Mycroft, informed that I was safe and well. I vaguely wondered whether Mycroft would be surprised to know that I had been smuggled into Tibet together with a consignment of arms – and by a British secret agent – or whether he had knowledge of some special purpose, such as Government business, which made it desirable for me to be here!

I recognized that if we were caught I could be treated as a spy. I wondered whether the real reason that Deng had given me the revolver was for my own personal use if I became in perilous danger of being caught!

Her Majesty Queen Victoria's Government appeared to be preparing the Tibetan people for an uprising should the necessity arise. They were obviously constantly aware of the 'Yellow Peril' and of the proximity of Tibet to the sub-continent of India. If the Chinese were able either to invade or take over control of Tibet by some other means, then the arming and training of an internal army of liberation seemed to me to be eminently necessary to protect the 'Jewel in the Crown' of the British Empire – India.

I questioned Deng about possible attacks on Tibet by the Chinese. He explained in his oddly concise English that Her Majesty's Government were afraid that the Chinese might seek to conquer Tibet as a stepping-stone to conquering Sikkim and Bengal. Bengal had the perfect climate for growing the opium poppy. He then went on to say that the East India Company, and Jardine Matheson & Dent, were shipping anything up to seven million pounds sterling's worth of opium annually to mainland China via Hong Kong. China officially disapproved of the barter of food and goods for the opium and would benefit enormously if they could annexe and destroy the poppy fields – hence the threat to Bengal which Tibetan resistance could avert.

'While Dalai Lama rules,' said Deng, 'no opium in Tibet. No Chinese threat to Bengal.'

I learned that normal traders tried to join up with other traders wherever possible in order to form such large caravans that *tchapas* were deterred from attacking them. We, on the other hand, were anxious to avoid other caravans because of my presence.

I felt the responsibility weigh heavily upon me, since I had desired to come to Tibet, on what could be construed as a mere whim, to consult with the Dalai Lama.

I deemed it incumbent upon me to learn Tibetan as fluently as possible if I were to enter Lhasa and meet the God-King and thereby justify the inconvenience to which I had put my companions.

We were, by now, passing through verdant valleys with irrigated fields surrounding dwellings. Here and there we saw inaccessible hermitages perched on high cliffs and hill-tops. The inevitable monastery sounded its *ragdongs* as soon as we were sighted, provoking instant replies from surrounding but distant lamaseries.

Streams and lakes abounded with fish which Deng, Bonjl and Tagstel caught by laying a weighted net on the stream bed. Cords were attached to the corners. The fish were lured over the net with *tsampa*. The men were adept at their task: two of them raising the edges of the net so that the fish could not escape while the third clubbed the fish to death.

They always took care to fish or hunt out of sight of lamaseries so as not to offend the Buddhist monks, who abhor the taking of any kind of life.

I was profoundly moved by the great silences that I experienced on the plains of Tibet. I have heard the sweet sound of a songbird lonely in such a silence until answered by a responding call, and as beautiful to listen to as the flute played by Da Vincenzo at the Albert Hall.

It was after such an occasion that I was moved to take out my fairly recently acquired violin and play the barcarole from *The Tales of Hoffmann*, albeit a trifle mournful air, to the wonder and astonishment of my companions. Two days later, when I again decided to scrape a smooth melody, I found that the bow was missing. I apologized profusely to my companions for not being able to entertain them but they took the news with good grace.

It was Wangdula's custom to travel from soon after dawn until midday and then to rest for two to three hours while the animals grazed. We used this period to make any necessary repairs or modifications to our clothing or equipment. We then resumed travel until an hour before dark before striking camp for the night. What was it Sheridan said? 'Oh what hypocrites are we who profess to love beauty and yet never see the dawn!'

Never have I seen so many consecutive dawns rise, lemon and pink, orange and dove-grey. Honesty compels me to admit my preference for ragged-bannered sunsets.

At every opportunity I learned Tibetan, much of it on the hoof, and I practised avidly on Deng and Lalam, both of whom were literally saddled with me.

We passed through valleys where the mineral outcrops were curiously carved by erosions and which sometimes hemmed us in menacingly. In these places we rode with our rifles cocked just in case of ambush by *tchapas*. We rode with our *khatas* wrapped around our lower faces to avoid inhaling a constant cloud of fine dust.

It was also in such confined spaces that the animals had sometimes to be relieved of their packs, which then had to be carried forward manually until the way was again wide enough for them to be reladen. I took my turn and I swear that I have never had such strong and wiry muscles before in the whole of my life; nor have I ached all over so much!

We had just struck camp and unloaded the beasts one evening when Tagstel yelled a warning. We all looked to where he pointed. Travelling the same track that we had just pulled off was a large dust cloud, golden in the last rays of the setting sun, and kicked up by a group of horsemen proceeding at speed.

Wangdula gave an order. His men reached for their rifles and took up defensive positions. Deng knelt beside them and I joined him without enthusiasm. I had been instructed on the use of my rifle and I had practised with live cartridges, in consequence of which I loathed rifles more than hitherto. I would have much preferred to use my revolver.

Wangdula observed the riders through his telescope.

As they approached I was alarmed when I saw that they were all wearing full face masks. I gripped my rifle firmly and was immediately glad that I knew how to use it. I took aim ready to fire when Wangdula should use the attack signal of 'Dal-thog hjug-pa'. I took them for a band of tchapas.

It was with considerable relief that I heard Wangdula call, 'Ya po re', and saw him rise to his feet. He snapped his telescope together and replaced his rifle into its saddle holster. We all stood.

The band of men rode into the grassy area where we had chosen to camp for the night. Beneath their tchombas they wore garnet-coloured pleated skirts, blue chemises and red velvet waistcoats. Two of the party were slightly more richly attired in similar clothing, but embroidered.

We had not had time to erect our tents and so there was nowhere for me to conceal myself.

Deng explained that they were monks who were travelling without ceremony. They wore masks to protect their faces from grit whipped up by their speeding mounts.

Some of the monks acted as servants, called chelas, to the two who were richly attired. They set up tents, lit fires of dried animal dung, and took the horses to drink at the nearby stream. All was done under the supervision of a superior monk.

Wangdula duly exchanged khatas with the supervising monk, who, like most of the others, had removed his mask. I was curious about the two lamas, who showed no sign of removing theirs. I caught them staring at me briefly but it did not disturb me. I was, after all, a stranger – a *phling* – in the Land of Snows and was bound, in my turn, to attract their curiosity.

I was more amused by the covert looks given to me by some of the monks, who seemed to me to be embarrassed by my presence. There was something in the lamas' mien – something furtive!

The next curious event was the refusal of the monks to identify either of their lamas or to divulge the name of their lamasery. Wangdula sat in a state of listless depression. I accepted the blame as, naturally, the monks were disgusted with him for allowing a *phling* to join his caravan.

The monks set up their camp a little distance from ours, and so we were able to talk around our fire without being overheard. Deng suggested that Wangdula should take the lamas gifts of crystallized fruits, sugar, salt and dried fruit from his merchandise in an effort to establish goodwill. This he did and his gifts were refused in a manner which, I was told, was most discourteous. Furthermore, he was told to abandon me to fate and my own devices, which he refused to do.

Wangdula refused all food. Not that we had much which Bonjl dare serve us. We dare not cook and eat the fish, which we had caught during our midday break, in such close proximity to the holy men. Instead we dined off *tsampa* – lightly roasted barley meal, raw onions, dried fruit, and Tibetan-style tea flavoured with salt and rancid butter.

This diet was totally foreign to me, so I boiled some water. I had the opportunity to test, and prove Boyle's and Charles's conclusion that water boils at a lower temperature at high

altitudes than it does at sea level. However, it was not long
before I was drinking the unpalatable hot water to settle my
colic.

CHAPTER 7

❦

I slept fitfully that night. I was mystified by the two lamas retaining their masks and steadfastly refusing to reveal their identities.

The monks woke me before dawn with their chanting of *'Om mani padme um'* which roughly translates as, 'Hail, jewel in the lotus'.

As dawn broke I pulled my *tchomba* around my shoulders to protect me from the cold air and wandered in the general direction of the monks' black tents. The *chelas* were busy strapping the distinctive Tibetan wooden saddles on to the restless horses, and dismantling and loading the tents on to packhorses. I stood and watched for a minute but they all studiously ignored me.

Behind me Bonjl brewed tea on an argol fire – a fire of dried dung – and the others of our party started loading the dzos. A morning ritual to which I had become very accustomed.

A patch of colour caught my attention and I walked away from both busy parties in that direction. I did not look back.

I came to a bank just beyond the now exhausted grazing. I found myself looking at a silver-grey leafed plant growing in profusion close to the ground. Its leaves were fringed with a contrasting blood-red colour. I dropped to my knees the better to inspect its beauty and as I did so something whizzed above my head. I looked up, expecting to see a bee or hornet but was startled to see an object spinning and sparkling and bouncing across the rough ground before me. From the sound of its deflection as it struck stones, it was evidently metallic.

I quickly looked over my shoulder, first at Wangdula's camp, but everyone appeared to be occupied, and then beyond to the monks' camp. There too everyone appeared to be occupied. No one looked in my direction.

Making my way to where I had last seen the object, I searched. At last I lit upon the object after due diligence.

I looked again at the two parties, first my own, and then at the monks. The monks were all in the saddle. One of the lamas looked directly at me. He stared through the slits in his mask with malevolence for a full half-minute before turning away and giving the signal to proceed at a trot. By chance both Wangdula and Bonjl were also looking in my direction. Wangdula turned away as Bonjl signalled that tea was ready.

Waiting until all of the monks were on their way, I picked up the object. It was a five-pointed star made up of wickedly sharp pointed blades. I took out my kerchief and wrapped my hand in it before taking the star carefully between finger and thumb. I remembered Blackburn's demonstration and was anxious not to destroy any finger ridge-prints there might be on it.

Who, I addressed the question to myself, had thrown this lethal missile? And what had motivated such an attack? Any one of the monks or lamas, or any one of my own party even, could have been the culprit. Wangdula perhaps? He had been depressed since his rejection by the lamas. He had lost face before his own men because he was accompanied by a *philing*. The monks had even churlishly rejected his gifts. Perhaps in his judgement his mistreatment justified my becoming a target for his hatred. I found that very hard to believe.

I walked back towards camp.

What if it had been one of the monks? That seemed to me to be far more likely. But would a devout Buddhist attempt to maim or kill another human being when his beliefs would not allow him to kill even an insect?

As I drank my tea I searched through my belongings and selected a box containing small cakes of tooth-cleaning compound, which I emptied on to the ground. I placed the star carefully into the empty box and closed the lid.

My companions were all but ready to leave when I remembered the cakes of tooth-cleaning compound. I decided to abandon them as I did not wish to draw attention to myself. Wangdula rode busily up and down the line of burdened animals inspecting them, his vigour seemingly restored. I placed my tea bowl in its bag and hung it around my neck together with the box containing the star.

I mounted my horse, took my packhorse by its lead-rein and rode to the rear end of the caravan. The beasts were already on the move, the geese honking indignantly at the rocking motion.

Wangdula took the van with Deng close behind him. Lobsang helped to keep the beasts moving while praying as he thumbed his rosary; he too had been upset by last night's events. Trethong used a stick to prod and whack the beasts rather than wasting his breath cajoling them. He turned and spat to leave his mark where the monks had camped.

Lalam recited poetry and shouted 'Hoi, hoi', at the beasts between each verse. Bonjl cracked a whip to urge the beasts along. Tagstel brought up the rear beside me with his bag of pebbles and his – oh so accurate – throwing. I gently delayed so that within a very short time there was no one at my back.

As we proceeded the fine dust cloud rose and entered our throats and nostrils. As was usual I wrapped my *khata* around the lower part of my face, otherwise, I knew, I would soon start coughing. I contemplated the cloud of fine dust and, on an impulse, I removed the throwing star from its box. Using my kerchief I held it carefully in the dust cloud and watched as, upon its shiny surface, a distinguishable and unmistakable right thumb-ridge print formed. That of my would-be assassin.

CHAPTER 8

◈

When we rested, I sat apart and sketched the loops and whorls of that thumb-ridge print in my journal. A tedious task but one made easier with the aid of my lens. For good measure I mirror-sketched it a second time, as the ridges would be seen on the actual thumb. I observed a crease or scar running part-way across the ridges. I compared the two sketches of those thumb-ridge prints and studied them so that they would remain indelibly in my memory. If I ever saw that thumb or ridge-print again...!

That done, I considered two mysteries. Who had thrown the star at me? The motive for such an action?

I was sceptical about one of my own party being the culprit. It seemed to me to be more likely to have been one of the monks, possibly that masked lama with the malignant stare, the memory of which even now burned in my brain. Could it have been he? If so, why? He had not even met me! By reporting my presence to the Men of Kham police force, he could ensure my arrest and eventual deportation. So why attempt to maim or kill me?

I resolved to compare each member of my party's right thumb-ridges with the sketch in my journal. Lobsang was religious and therefore superstitious and so I broached the subject with him by telling him of my interest in good-fortune thumbs. That appealed to him. He allowed me to sketch his right thumb-ridges in my journal. The thumb-ridge print on the throwing star was not his.

Later that day I easily persuaded Bonjl to allow me to sketch his right thumb-ridge in my journal. I was not surprised to perceive that he too was not the culprit. Indeed, I would have been shocked to find that either of them had attempted to take my life.

The exercise also helped me to broaden my grasp of the Tibetan language.

That night I again slept fitfully under canvas, ever uncertain that I might be subjected to another attack; my instincts for self-preservation urging me to listen and to analyse sounds – ready for the dagger to pierce the tent canvas – and my muscles flexed ready to roll away from the assassin's thrust.

When I rose next morning I remained close to the fringe of our camp, where it would be difficult for anyone to hurl a missile at me.

During that day I sketched Trethong's and Lalam's right thumb-ridges in my journal, and eliminated them from my enquiries, as I was wont to say to Watson.

Deng had noticed me taking sketches, so I confided to him what had happened. I also explained the purpose of the sketches and showed him the throwing-star weapon.

'You waste your time,' he said. 'That is Chinese weapon.' He cocked his head in puzzlement. 'Thrown by monk?'

'Or lama?' I queried.

From the fleeting unguarded expression which came and

went in the blink of an eye to Deng's otherwise inscrutable face, I knew that he was in possession of some knowledge which he chose to keep to himself. 'You are in no danger from Wangdula or any of us,' he said.

Deng must have seen a fleeting expression on my face.

'Satisfy yourself. Take sketch of my ridges and add to your collection. Tomorrow ask Wangdula and Tagstel to give theirs.'

I slept more easily that night and was relieved to find that my last two companions' ridges were different from those on the star when I sketched them on the following day.

My lungs had become acclimatized to the somewhat rarefied air at the height of about 10,000 feet at which we travelled and, as I was faced with a three-pipe mystery, I lit up and contemplated.

Now that there was absolutely no doubt that one of the monks or lamas had hurled that star missile at me I was narrowing my field of research. I work on the principle that when all else has been eliminated the only conclusion, no matter how improbable, must be the solution.

I dismissed the gharry driver in Calcutta as too remote to have passed on information of my whereabouts. I came to the conclusion, painfully but firmly, that the couple in the *gompa* had shown my cigarette case to one of the monks or lamas. That person had found that piece of my visiting card which bore my name, and so must be able to read English, and must be aware of my reputation. That, coupled with the statement that I was a magician summoned to assist the Dalai Lama, had resulted in the attempt on my life. That person had wrongfully assumed that I had been summoned to investigate something – but what? A crime? The answer to that eluded me, but it was obvious that that person, as yet unknown, had probably committed a criminal act, so heinous that he was prepared to murder to ensure that he remained undetected as the culprit.

I was torn between two possibilities for my quarry: the lama who had stared at me from behind his mask, and the senior monk because he was, without doubt, Chinese.

CHAPTER 9

✑

W̶e continued our journey, the Himalaya range now far behind us, and we decided from then on that on all occasions when we met people or passed near to lamaseries or villages I would adopt a stooping posture to disguise my height. I would also wear a piece of cloth over my head as a cowl to conceal my face – albeit now somewhat weather-beaten and a colour between ruddy and brown.

I had the opportunity to observe much of the fauna of Tibet, from marmots, which we shot and ate on several occasions, to wild sheep, goats and kiangs – the wild asses of Tibet. I also observed the inhabitants from afar. Many of the men were working in the fields, harvesting root crops, and, on one particularly hot 'Indian Summer' day, women were working bare-breasted beside them.

With hindsight, I suppose such a hot day was not so surprising in a latitude south of Cairo.

The whole country was medieval, with its ancient practices, star-shaped crenellated towers, and square-shaped villages, so arranged the better to resist attack and siege.

Both Deng and Tagstel could sight a group of travellers or a caravan from a long way off. Wangdula's telescope then came into play as he endeavoured to identify the occupation or type of people approaching, and to judge whether our paths were likely to cross. This gave me ample time to assume my disguise.

On several occasions we met groups of monks wearing the tall, coloured hats which denoted their sect and rank. The abbot or lama would invariably be riding the finest horse or be being carried in a sedan-chair.

That made me realize that the group of monks with my would-be assassin amongst them had not worn their hats. They had taken care not even to allow us that clue as to their identities or monastery.

We descended to nearer 9,000 feet, still avoiding contact with travellers wherever possible, and reached undulating grassland. We were on a plateau at that level when Tagstel pointed out a group of horsemen in the distance, travelling in the opposite direction.

Tagstel called to Wangdula. Wangdula was studying the group through his telescope when they wheeled and were returning, at a gentle pace parallel to us, whence they had come. I heard the term *tchapas* being used. However, their pace turned into a trot and then into a canter and the group soon faded into the distance. I noted the looks of relief on both Wangdula's and Tagstel's faces. Our caravan continued in the direction the group had taken.

Bonjl had gathered wild onions on our descent and that night we dined on spit-roast chickens and the pungent vegetable.

The plain we travelled across on the following day was covered in a stiff grass turned yellow and brown as autumn approached. It hardly bent in a slight breeze and so even its inclined height was still above the knee. I was surprised that there was no habitation or herdsmen attending their dzos or cattle: we were instantly on our guard, instinct telling us that all was not as it should be.

Tagstel shielded his eyes and pointed out something ahead. Wangdula trained his telescope on it. At first I could hardly see it but, as the caravan lumbered along, a group of horses became discernible. Wangdula called a halt so that we could consider the most appropriate course of action to take. Deciding that the horses were tethered we looked for their riders but without success. Nevertheless, the sight was intimidating and so barred our progress to Lhasa.

Wangdula, Tagstel and Deng conferred. The animals took the opportunity to graze on what little green grass they could find. Yaks need to stop to feed whilst dzos have the advantage of being able to graze while on the move.

The three of them came to the conclusion that there was a *tchapa* ambush ahead. We remembered the group of the previous day. Wangdula expected a demand for tribute in exchange for allowing the caravan to pass safely on its journey, but no such demand came.

It would be unwise to press on and it would be inconvenient to take a wide detour. Anyway, had we done so, the *tchapas* had only to mount their horses and either try to frighten us into offering tribute, or openly to attack us. The only advantage about the latter strategy would be in making the *tchapas* show themselves when they mounted their horses to pursue us. In that event they would at least become targets, even though moving ones, instead of being completely invisible, as they were now.

We were all uncomfortably aware that we had no idea of

the *tchapas'* positions. The deep grass showed no obvious indentations as it gently flowed and rippled in the light breeze. Although it was unlikely that the *tchapas* would be far away from their horses, we all scrutinized the surrounding grass nervously, and held our rifles at the ready.

Reluctantly, Wangdula and Deng, their chests criss-crossed with ammunition belts came to the only sensible decision open to us. As there appeared to be about a score of horses the corresponding number of *tchapas* meant that we were outnumbered. As we could not see the *tchapas* to exchange fire with them we would have to shoot their mounts. Regrettable but necessary.

Wangdula, Deng, Tagstel and Lalam dismounted and crawled through the grass. For a time the four of us who remained mounted lost sight of them and we kept a nervous watch around us.

The geese were no noisier than usual, which was a comfort.

Suddenly, as though at a prearranged signal, four shots rang out and three horses keeled over. The sound did not come from the direction which I had expected. We saw our comrades' heads briefly emerge, shots rang out again and two more horses fell. The four men had not crawled in a straight line towards the tethered horses, but were nearer to them and much further away from us than I would have thought possible. There was method in their actions. The remainder of the horses panicked and pulled at their tethers. That resulted in the *tchapas* being flushed from their places of concealment, rushing to the horses, releasing their tethers and mounting them. Five doubled up.

Meanwhile, the four of us left behind took aim but held our fire.

The *tchapas* fired wildly in our direction as they took flight.

We continued to hold our fire for fear of inadvertently shooting our companions. They, in their turn, held their fire, and remained hidden in the grass.

The sound of the *tchapas'* gunfire did not have the sharp 'crack' of the rifles of our party. Trethong ejected a stream of red spittle in contempt. He nodded his head in disdain and said something in Tibetan. I caught the word 'bad' and, as I had noted that no *tchapa* bullets had whizzed around us, I reasoned that Trethong had remarked something about bad gunpowder. We'd been in no real danger. Despite that, Trethong fired over the *tchapas'* heads to deter them from any further thoughts of attack. They rode off at speed in the direction we were taking with much shaking of fists and cries of anguish.

Some time later, when I looked back, the lammergeyers and other vultures were circling above their feast. We too dined off cheval steaks that evening. Bonjl had that quality of a good cook: never to waste good food.

CHAPTER 10

❦

O
ur journey continued across the grassy plain for
another day. Grazing was patchy but ample. Wangdula
was convinced that the *tchapas* would strike again, and next
time it would be from some vantage point.

We came to the edge of the grassland, where some ancient
river had plunged over the side of the plateau, leaving a
deep dry channel. This was to be our way down to the valley
below, where the mighty Brahmaputra River flowed. There
was no other way, but it was the ideal place in which to
spring an ambush. We discussed our plan of action.

Wangdula still expected that, as normal, we would have
warning shots fired over our heads, then the *tchapas* would
parley over our ransom before allowing us to continue on our
way. As we had killed five of their horses, the ransom was
likely to be a high one and might even include five of our
horses.

Deng had misgivings. Some instinct perhaps? 'Check your
firearms, Herr Sigerson,' he told me. He reached into his
saddlebag and took out the two hand grenades that he had
removed from the yak's load. He hung them from his belt.

Determined not to be caught off our guard, we each

checked our firearms and made sure that they were fully loaded. I felt the comforting weight of my revolver in my webbing belt. I noticed Lobsang praying and thumbing his rosary and touching his large *gaou* for good luck.

We all dismounted and proceeded, bridles resting on our arms and our mounts' muzzles pushing gently into the small of our backs to give us protection from a rear attack. Wangdula acted as vanguard.

Trethong walked immediately behind Wangdula. A third of the way along the caravan were Bonjl and Lobsang; at the two-thirds position came Deng and me, and last of all came Lalam and Tagstel as rearguard.

The two yaks in front of Wangdula made the gully seem narrow, their loads nearly touching the steep sides in places. The rest of the beasts barged between us, in pairs and knocking their loads together, panting and snorting. I swear that I could smell fear mixed with animal odours in that confined space.

As we proceeded the sides of the deep channel rose like cliffs on both sides of us, menacing, overhanging, threatening, and my mouth became as dry as the ancient river bed we trod. We had all removed our hats so that our field of vision upward would not be impaired. Our progress seemed strangely silent with no cries of, 'Hoi, hoi,' or the crack of a whip.

Suddenly shots sounded ahead of Deng and me, the reports muffled so that they seemed a long way off. Movement above us and to our left preceded further gunfire but we had instinctively flung ourselves to the left to be shielded from the assailants above.

Deng crouched beside me, alert, tensed, ready.

A *tchapa* behind a rock above the opposite side of the gully levelled his musket at me. The explosive round from Deng's rifle in the confined space made me jump. I saw my would-be assassin slump. Then several more shots rang out from Deng's rifle.

More shots with that strange muffled sound came from above with the *tchapas'* bullets ricocheting off the gully walls, and I heard bellows of fear and pain.

The sounds of a yak in pain were the loudest, and its bellowing mingled with the sounds of gunfire from both in front of me and behind me. The sound of gunfire became more wild and bullets flew about indiscriminately.

A *tchapa* fell into the gully from directly above, bleeding from his side but clutching a sabre. He raised himself on one elbow but before he could lunge at Deng, I shot him in the mouth with my revolver. The *tchapa* dropped back, dead.

Deng lobbed a grenade with vigour, his arm sweeping over his head to hurl it on to the rocky position above. The explosion quelled all opposition from that area. Rocks and bloody fragments landed in the trench.

We were no longer pinned down by firing from above but were still unable to move. The beasts had not remained docile during this exchange but had stampeded, following their leaders down the gorge.

Onward they lumbered, past Deng and me and frustrating any sniper's bullet from above. And then came the most extraordinary sight: Tagstel following in their wake, standing in the saddle, like a circus performer, and firing his rifle from his elevated position. He was followed by Lalam covering his back and running, weaving, dodging and firing his rifle. Deng and I joined him, turning from side to side, taking pot shots at any suggestion of movement above us from the banks of the gully.

We had to skirt a fallen yak and just beyond it lay Lobsang. Bonjl was cushioning his head. Deng and I stopped beside them. While Deng watched and gave cover, I felt Lobsang's pulse. It was strong. His eyes flickered and opened. He focused them on us. 'Am I dead?' he asked in Tibetan. Deng translated. Lobsang then clutched at his large *gaou*. I could see no sign of a wound but his head was bleeding from where he must have fallen back on to a rock. Then Lobsang moved his hand and I perceived a deep groove in his *gaou*. A bullet must have been deflected by it.

'*Ya po re*,' I reassured him.

Deng and Bonjl helped Lobsang to his feet. By now the four of us were on our own. We crouched warily before we risked following the panicked caravan. As we made progress the dust thinned and we became aware of the silence.

That silence was punctuated by groans of the wounded *tchapas* and then gunshots, which silenced them. The pungent smell of cordite clung to my clothing.

Then there came the sound of hoofs approaching from the lower part of the gully. We tensed, our weapons ready. Trethong hove into view, relief enveloping his normally inscrutable features as he espied us.

'It's all over. They've been beaten off!' he exclaimed. Deng translated.

We walked gently down the gully to where it opened in to the valley below. Wangdula and Tagstel were nowhere to be seen. Lalam was busy gently coaxing the beasts into a group. We four found our horses, then we assisted Lalam in unloading the yaks and dzos and examining them for bullet wounds or other injuries sustained in the mêlée.

Trethong meanwhile kept watch.

A scream echoed from the cliff overhanging the valley.

'What was that?' I exclaimed.

'*Tchapas* not after Wangdula's goods or ransom,' Deng said. 'Man you shot Chinese, not Tibetan.'

In the heat of the skirmish I had noticed that, but any significance had escaped me. Before I could reply, Deng continued, 'They sent to kill you!'

We both looked in the direction of the cliff overhanging the gully as another scream rent the air.

'Survivor telling who paid to assassinate you,' Deng added laconically.

We continued rounding up the beasts and treating them for abrasions. From the neat bullet holes in some of their loads I realized that several would have been dead if they had not carried their own protection. Lobsang worked cheerfully, enthusiastically, and with a satisfied smile beaming at all of us. Had he not paid five whole *sangs* for that largest of *gaous*, and had it not saved his life, he repeatedly reminded us. And had not Herr Sigerson read his right thumb-ridges and told him what a lucky man he was?

While we worked we heard further screams, then silence.

All of the beasts had been relieved of their loads, their grazes treated, then they'd been hobbled and were grazing by the time Wangdula and Tagstel returned. They were trailing six horses on lead reins.

'Eleven. All dead,' stated Wangdula flatly. 'There are more but we didn't count the pieces.' He looked at Deng.

'Two, I think. That makes thirteen.'

I then understood why Deng had chosen Wangdula. His many qualities included hatred of the Chinese, which had been amply demonstrated within the last few hours.

'We ready for them. Knew they would attack. Good rifles, good cartridges. Against their poor gunpowder!' Wangdula turned to Deng. 'With such weapons we defend Tibet from Chinese desire for our homeland.'

'Who sent them?' asked Deng quietly.

'Poo Shih Foo, Steward of Abbot Surkhang Gyadze,' Wangdula replied.

Deng looked at me thoughtfully.

'You know them?' I asked.

'The throwing star!' Deng paused. 'Poo Shih Foo is Chinese. He probably threw it. And ...' he nodded, 'yes, I feel sure one of masked lamas was Gyadze himself!'

CHAPTER 11

&

W e rested for two days and dined off yak steaks.
I had time to char some twigs in order to mix the
powdered charcoal with salt with which to clean my teeth.
When I was a boy, the servants used either powdered chalk
or a mixture of soot and salt to clean their teeth – something
my mother used to insist upon. I now regretted abandoning
the cakes of tooth-cleansing compound on the day when the
star was thrown at me.

Wangdula, Trethong, Lobsang and Lalam performed the
gruesome task of hacking the bodies of the dead Chinese into
pieces. Tibetans rarely bury their dead. Instead, they
dismember them and leave them for the lammergeyers and
other vultures to consume.

The beasts needed to rest. Some had quite nasty abrasions, and Wangdula wanted these to develop scabs for
protection before we proceeded further.

We were fortunate in having added six horses to our
caravan, as they would carry the dead yak's burden under a
skilful redistribution of loads. The dead men's weapons
would sell in Lhasa market. The horses would also help to
lighten the loads of two injured dzos.

The bodies of the dead had been stripped before being dismembered. Bonjl thoroughly washed the clothing in the stream beside which we were camped. He spread the clothing out to dry on rocks and scrub. We all took the opportunity to bathe and to change into clean clothing as far as we were able.

After the two days' rest, we pressed on towards the Brahmaputra River.

During our midday rests Bonjl acted as tailor and cut up two pairs of trousers stripped off the Chinese. He then proceeded to sew them together again as one pair. He lengthened the legs so that the modified trousers would fit me. Then he performed a similar service using the largest tunic, letting in a panel across the back, lengthening it, and the sleeves, and patching the bullet hole.

Wangdula insisted that I must be dressed in Tibetan style from now on, even beneath my *tchomba*.

One day we entered a wide valley in which a herd of yak were grazing. Near by was a group of what appeared to be giant spiders. As we drew closer I was amazed to see that they were black yak-hide tents. Deng explained that they had no interior support poles and were unique to Tibet. Props were driven into the ground around the tents, then pulley ropes made of yak hair were stretched over these props. These ropes were then fastened to pegs which were hammered into the ground a good distance from the props. The tent roof was then suspended in air and an apron attached to its edge formed the outer wall.

Their herdsmen inhabitants wore large silver earrings and a skin garment slung over one shoulder, leaving the other bare. Their women wore silver trinkets in their hair, and a sort of fork slung across the front of their abdomens which served to support the leather buckets they were using to catch yaks' milk.

I had to observe them from the anonymity of my cowl.

Eventually we had to join the main highway of compacted earth to Lhasa. We crossed the solid timber bridge over the mighty Brahmaputra. As we did so we also joined the mainstream of pilgrims and other travellers making their way to Lhasa. I was forced to stoop and to wear my cowl more frequently.

Lamaseries, convents, villages and small towns now abounded. Prayer flags fluttered from wayside bushes.

We came across people chattering, chanting and clattering their hand-held prayer wheels. In competition were the raucous cries of crows, daws and cranes, as well as the familiar sounds of cymbals, drums and *ragdongs* from the monasteries around us.

I enquired of Deng what he knew of Surkhang Gyadze.

'He is abbot of Tengyeling Monastery, outside Lhasa. He very progressive, with strong leaning towards all things Chinese. He not popular lama but is confidant of His Holiness, the Dalai Lama.'

'Is that all you can tell me about him?'

'Yes. I think so. What you want to know?'

I remember placing my fingertips together – a habit I have – while I gathered my thoughts. 'Is he, for instance, well-travelled?'

'I believe he is.'

'China?'

'Undoubtedly. He preaches peace between Tibetans and Chinese.'

'Surely, that is no bad thing?'

'It is,' retorted Deng sharply, 'if, in order to enjoy peace, Tibetans have to bow to will of Chinese Emperor!'

'Has Gyadze by any chance lived in India? Somewhere where he would have learned the English language?'

'Probably. Gyadze much travelled.'

Deng listened with interest as I related my belief that someone, maybe Gyadze, had read my name inside my cigarette case and was probably aware of my reputation.

'As explorer?'

'No. I have misled you. My real name is Sherlock Holmes. The reputation I have is of a highly successful consultant detective.'

Deng shrugged.

'You knew all along?'

He shrugged again. 'I know many things. Guess others.'

CHAPTER 12

∽

Deng and I made plans against eventualities.

My height made me stand out amongst my companions, and my facial characteristics and skin colour labelled me instantly as a *philing*, whereas Deng was a northern Nepalese and regarded as Tibetan. He told me that he had relatives in Lhasa and that he himself had lived there. He spoke the language fluently.

I think we both knew from past experience the perils which I presented, and felt alarm at the hostility I could attract, which could endanger the whole party.

Apart from the aristocracy of the country, the class system comprises coolies and peasants on the lowest scale; then merchants, traders and herdsmen who are equivalent to the British middle class; and above these nuns, monks and lamas, a privileged upper class who wield power from their position of spiritual respect. I decided to adopt the pose of a peasant.

By stooping and carrying a light bundle on my back, I adopted a posture that concealed my height, and my cowl fell forward, concealing my face. It was indeed a painful decision, as it is no joke when a tall man has to take a foot off his stature.

It had become evident to me that there was no kind of wheeled transport in Tibet. Everything was transported on beasts of burden or on the heads of peasants or on their backs. Everyone according to his or her station travelled on foot, by litter or sedan chair, or on a donkey or horse.

As we had deemed it the safest and most prudent ploy for me to pose as a peasant, I found myself travelling more and more on foot, as befitted that station. With increasing frequency persons passed us, coming from or travelling to the Holy City.

I experimented with my crude pigments to colour my face. I would have to blend in with the Tibetan coolies when I reached the Forbidden City.

In the meantime I was content to wear the hood to conceal me from curious eyes.

We were all wary of the occasional Man of Kham whom we came across in case they had been alerted to intercept me. I would then lag behind Wangdula's caravan. If I was discovered we reasoned that my arrest would satisfy the authorities and so my companions and their contraband would be ignored.

About half a day's journey from Lhasa we camped and Wangdula and Tagstel rode into the city.

They returned next day reporting that the Tibetan police were manning the city gates in strength. Two days later four men rode into our camp. They had twelve yaks loaded with reeds and thatching. Within minutes they left with Wangdula's eleven yaks and four of the Chinese *tchapas'* horses and their weapons.

Deng released his penultimate homing pigeon with a message attached to its leg and his usual, 'Beware of hawks, friend of soldiers.'

I shook my head in a way which indicated my doubt.

'I merely obey orders,' stated Deng.

At dawn on the following day Deng and I rode ahead of Wangdula's animal train. We had concluded that the Tibetan police were specifically looking out for me. That would be the reason for their being in strength. Perhaps Chinese so-called diplomats would be on the lookout for me too? If I were to elude them a certain element of surprise would be necessary. My disguise as a peasant, I hoped, would get me unobserved into Lhasa.

Wangdula and Tagstel's reconnaissance had primarily been to enable them safely to pass on the weapons and ammunition. However, it seemed that it had served a secondary purpose in advising me just how difficult it was going to be to enter Lhasa undetected. But that I was determined to do!

Wangdula and Tagstel had entered by the west gate, as if they had travelled from the Tibetan interior. Today, Deng and I would attempt to enter via the south gate across the Rainbow Bridge spanning the Kyi River. This was the gate through which Wangdula's caravan would enter Lhasa.

We tethered our horses by the highway where Wangdula would find them later in the day, and where they were in reach of plentiful grazing and water to sustain them. Deng and I carried noisome burdens of kindling sticks and dried animal dung about another half-mile, walking off the highway but alongside it.

We eventually took cover in a ditch from where we could observe the highway. We had seen very few people at that early hour and, perversely, after seeking to avoid people for so long, we now needed to join a group of people and become a part of a crowd.

I coloured my hands and forearms, neck, ears and face. Deng tinted around my eyes. By now I could understand and speak a satisfactory vocabulary of the Tibetan language.

With my indigenous apparel, my back bent beneath my load, I was confident that I could pass as a peasant. With the cowl or hood to cover my profile I knew that I had done my utmost to disguise myself. The outcome rested in the hand of fate.

I am not, by nature, an early riser, and so I took the opportunity to have an uncustomary nap, there in the ditch, while Deng kept watch.

It was mid morning when Deng judged that an approaching band of pilgrims would be large enough in which to merge ourselves. We threw dust over each other's clothes, took up our bundles on our backs and entered the throng. Deng pushed on ahead rather than be near me for his own safety, in case I was detected.

In any case I could not walk as fast as he. To take a foot off my height incurred much self-control and not a few aches and pains. Not that I complained. The burden was genuine on this occasion and weighed me down enough to convince even the most suspicious of policemen.

We were joined by a train of beasts carrying a trader's wares, and I became worried for a time that I might have miscalculated the timing and that Wangdula's caravan might merge with us. In the event, my fears were unnecessary.

Between the chanting of '*Om mani padme um*' people tried to strike up a conversation with me in my guise as a deformed coolie. I countered with, '*Kale, kale,*' the Tibetan equivalent of 'goodbye', and forged on a bit despite my painfully curved back.

All around me prayer wheels clicked in the hands of the faithful, and many pilgrims carried twigs to which were tied prayer flags. I wondered vaguely whether I would be expected to carry a prayer flag. I hoped not, but I was uncomfortably aware that I was ignorant of whether a peasant would customarily be expected to carry one. After all, I was not masquerading as a pilgrim.

As we approached the Rainbow Bridge the chanting of the faithful grew in volume. I peered from beneath my cowl to see Men of Kham at their business of scrutinizing everyone as they passed across the bridge over the Kyi Chu. Two Chinese men in long flowing mandarin robes stood at the far end of the bridge. I felt a chill pass up my spine.

I assumed that by now Deng had probably safely crossed the bridge and would be in the Forbidden City of Lhasa. At least he would be safe if I were detected. As a last resort there was always my revolver. The pilgrims continued with their chanting and I joined in with them.

The police seemed to be looking directly into the face of everyone who passed them, so I kept my face averted to the ground. The smell of human bodies and animals on that confined bridge almost made me retch. I sensed one Man of Kham trying to get a closer look at my face. He had to peer through the spaces between the people walking beside me. I bent even lower to frustrate him. He stepped towards me as if to enter the throng and I thought I had been detected. My heart seemed to stop beating. I experienced a timeless moment. All that I heard was the clacking of the prayer wheels around me, mingled with the wild cries of cranes flying overhead. At that instant a cry of '*Dal-thog hjing-pa*' went up from behind me and the Man of Kham stepped back, allowing me to pass.

As I crossed the Rainbow Bridge the two Chinese officials' attention was centred on what was going on behind me, and so they ignored my struggles to carry my load. I resisted the temptation to look back.

Proceeding ahead along the Mani Kashta Road, as directed by Deng and Wangdula, I travelled some distance to where the road begins to curve, before daring to take a sly look behind me. Everyone, or so it seemed, was at the bridge gawping. I deposited my burden and shielded my eyes against the sun's glare, the better to see, if possible, the reason for the cry that went up, and which, I later felt sure, saved my life.

I saw a group of policemen carrying their seven-foot-long staves with Wangdula's caravan and there was a lot of arm movement and gesticulating. Evidently Wangdula's caravan had all but caught up with me. I guessed my loyal party would be explaining the direction they thought I had taken. We had agreed that in such an event, they would hint at my heading for the North Gate.

I picked up my burden and continued on my way between the houses which lined the road. Some houses were built in terraces, others were detached, and some were two or three storeys high. They were built in wood and stone, with thatched and shingled shallow sloping roofs which curved upwards at the eaves and hips to throw off evil spirits which might slide down them!

Between the houses and above their jagged roof-line I perceived mature yellow-leaved poplars, more houses, and the occasional taller building.

Ahead of me appeared the *chorten* that I had been instructed to locate. This *chorten*, quite a high, bulbous tower, lay at the junction of the Mani Kashta and Lingkor roads, where Deng and I should meet.

CHAPTER 13

I love the bustle of cities, the diversity of their citizens, the opportunity to hear a world-renowned musician perform at an elegant concert hall, to hear the rattles and creaks of carriage springs, omnibuses, traps and Hansom cabs. The street vendors never fail to fascinate me with their inventive cries, colourful hand-carts or trays of all manner of foods and wares. I am amused too by the young boys who show initiative by patrolling the thoroughfares looking for fresh horse droppings to shovel up into buckets, and then sell to householders as manure for their gardens. Living in London I most of all eagerly await the newsvendors' cry at each fresh edition of the daily newspapers. For a mere copper, I could ascertain whether a crime had been committed that would merit my methods of deduction to solve mysteries of motive and the identity of the perpetrator.

Lhasa was different.

Here, no wheels rattled on the compacted dirt roads, no carriage-spring creaked. Instead, prayer wheels clacked in the hands of gently walking devout men and women. Donkeys and horses carried the more affluent, and beasts of burden transported food and merchandise to the market place. Lhasa had a completely different smell from London.

The aroma of incense burning at the base of the *chorten*

filled the air as I approached. Seated between the astrologer and the incense and gaou-pedlar was Deng.

He rose as I approached. We turned together into the Lingkor Road and walked eastward. Ahead of us in the distance was another *chorten* and between the strange houses I caught a glimpse of the variously shaped finials of other *chortens*; some monuments and some shrines.

'They make thorough search,' said Deng, and I saw the look of anxiety leave his face. 'I was afraid you would be detected and caught.'

'It was a near thing.' I went on to explain how Wangdula had unwittingly saved me. 'Where does the Lingkor Road lead?' I asked.

'It rings city,' Deng explained. 'Many important people have house along it.' He gestured to a building on our left which we were approaching. It was set behind a high wall and so we veered towards the centre of the road in order to see it better. 'It is Chinese mission.'

The sound of a horse's hoofs approaching at the gallop cut short anything else Deng was about to tell me.

We moved to the side of the road back towards the mission entrance gate. The horse rider yelled a warning. Deng shot out his hand to push me back. The rider wheeled, knocking Deng flying.

The rider's dark-brown *tchomba* was pushed aside by the collision to reveal a flash of yellow material beneath.

The gates of the mission were closed with a thud by unseen hands behind the horseman.

I shed my burden and helped Deng regain his feet, at the same time eliciting that he was not hurt, and knocking dry animal dung from his clothing.

A long yellow thread had caught on the scabbard of Deng's kukri. It must have come from the rider's clothing. I plucked it from Deng's person. His eyes narrowed with horror at the sight of that thread.

'Come quickly. We must go from here!'

We hurriedly resumed our journey and turned left at the first side road towards the centre of the city.

'That,' said Deng, 'was Gyadze.' He rubbed his hand across his chin from side to side. 'Hide that quickly.' His eyes indicated the thread which I still held. I put it into my notecase which I now wore in a bag suspended on a cord around my neck.

We had skirted the walls of the mission and I now looked back and across to the rear of the building. It was a buff stone solid structure beneath a terracotta tiled roof with curved eaves, and stood in its own grounds. At the rear of the building was a tree which is peculiar to Tibet. It had a stunted trunk from which branches protruded at right angles only to change direction suddenly, just as the limbs and hands of Tibetan dancers do so expressively.

Ours was a hurried walk until we were well beyond sight of the Chinese mission, then we slowed to a stroll. I was still carrying my burden and wished to be rid of it as soon as possible.

'You are certain that was Gyadze?'

'Certain.'

'You have seen him before?'

'Oh yes. Last time I in Lhasa. He becoming more influential and preaching greater links with Chinese.'

'But surely that is not popular with Tibetans? You told me yourself that Tibetans are fervent nationalists!'

'True, but Bon Pos, those who practise ancient religion,

and their shamans, have lost influence because of conversion of masses to Buddhism. They support Gyadze's views because they are of opinion that former followers would return to Bon worship if His Holiness Dalai Lama were to relinquish his supreme authority.'

'But Gyadze himself is a Buddhist lama!'

'He human and fallible,' stated Deng. 'Possibly motivated by desire for luxuries of life. Wealth and women!'

I waved my free hand impatiently to indicate that I understood. 'But the concern I detected on your face, Deng; there is something more?'

Deng held his silence.

'What is the significance of the yellow thread?'

'In Tibet,' said Deng slowly, 'only Dalai Lama allowed to wear yellow.'

'But Gyadze was wearing a yellow robe! I saw a flash of it beneath his *tchomba* as he bowled you over.'

Deng nodded his head wonderingly. 'Either Gyadze has delusions of grandeur or ...'

'Or?' I echoed.

'From what I've heard about you, Mr Holmes, you very man to find out alternative.'

As we proceeded Deng pointed out landmarks. To our right and in a north-easterly direction the decorated stonework and corner finials of the Jokhang Temple rose above the rooftops and groves of poplars.

In a north-westerly direction and on high ground to our left stood the Chakpori, the combined monastery and medical university with yellow stone castellated walls.

Further away and behind the Chakpori, the tiered white and dark red walls and flat roofs at several heights of the

Potala, the God-King's palace, soared above Lhasa against the background of far-off dusty grey hills.

Houses continued to line the road on our right but on our left buildings gave way to scrub in which stood a *chorten* then the scrub gave way to marsh adjoining the river Kyi. The Potala Palace came into view more clearly with the houses of the district of Sho crowding round its base.

Across the marsh and spanning the river, not too far away, was the Turquoise Bridge and close to it, Wangdula's home.

We decided to lie low for the remainder of the day. I was glad to shed my load although I would have to take it with me when the sun went down. To abandon it could provide the clue of how I had penetrated Lhasa.

The marsh area was dry enough for us to find suitable cover. Our only companions were tethered goats. Prayer flags fluttered from bushes. Distant chanting and the sounds of *Ragdongs* came on the still air from time to time. On several occasions pilgrims could be heard chanting and clacking their prayer wheels. Yaks bellowed beneath their burdens and as protest at the use of short whips some drovers used to urge them onwards.

Just before sunset we heard Lobsang's familiar *'Hoi, hoi, ya, ya.'* We watched from the cover of the reeds as Wangdula's caravan made its way towards Wangdula's home, the sun shining redly off Lobsang's large life-saving *gaou*. The beasts snorted and the two remaining geese honked their discomfort. Deng and I looked at each other; we each knew instinctively that the other was thinking that Wangdula had had a hard time convincing the Men of Kham of his innocence. My Western clothes and possessions were still in his care and those alone could have given the game away. Mind you, Wangdula was resourceful and would not have been above saying that he'd either found them or had been left with them when the *philing* abandoned him.

We watched the sun go down. Darkness and silence descended together.

We then set off for the Mani Lhakmang road, the thoroughfare on which Wangdula has his home. We turned left into that road and took extra care to make sure that no Men of Kham or Chinese were stationed there to intercept us.

Deng led me to a three-storey house with a wide gateway entrance and a courtyard beyond. We passed quickly through the gateway. Surrounding the yard were extensive stabling and barns, all dimly lit by butter lamps.

In the porchway into the house sat Lobsang in the lotus position in meditation; his rosary lay still between his fingers. He started at our approach. He sighed with relief, '*Ya po re.*' He placed his hand on his *gaou*, 'I prayed that good fortune would shine upon you.' For some curious reason I was able to understand what he said. He took my load from me and set it aside. Lobsang indicated for us to follow him.

Once indoors we exchanged our boots for woollen shoes, a selection of which awaited all guests.

After Deng and I had washed and changed, Wangdula introduced his wife Langel to me and we all four exchanged *khatas* in the observance of etiquette. I was conscious of my stubble as it had been early when I had had a cold-water shave.

Langel was then perhaps thirty with a handsome, round and readily smiling face. Her black hair was parted down the centre, and on either side she wore plaits which reached down to her waist. Into her glossy black hair were woven equally shiny silver ornaments. Silver earrings were suspended from her earlobes and across her head she was wearing a headdress of silver and turquoise. She was nearly as tall as Wangdula. Her bare arms were plump and she wore a dress of black brocade patterned with bright blue and white. On her feet she wore black woollen shoes.

Deng and I gave Langel boxes of Indian sweetmeats and exchanged polite conversation.

I felt somewhat self-conscious as I had had to scrub myself to remove the pigment from my skin and as a result I now had a somewhat ruddy complexion. I had donned Western dress for the first time since our second brush with the Chinese *tchapas*.

Langel had a homecoming feast prepared.

The nine of us, that is Wangdula and Langel, Bonjl, Lalam, Lobsang, Trethong, Tagstel, Deng and I sat down together. We were served by Yongyu, Wangdula and Langel's cook and maid.

I was aware of Langel's covert glances at me.

We dined on a thick vegetable soup. That was followed by two roast geese with apple and cinnamon sauce, accompanied by mixed vegetables in a creamy sauce and covered by a thick crust of grilled cheese. We drank beer with our meal, and finished with nuts and dried fruits, and tea laced with salt and rancid butter. I was amused to observe that Wangdula had his tea in his cup with the lid and saucer to accompany it. The rest of us had our lids set aside. Wangdula was, after all, the superior to all the rest of us, in his own home.

A cheerful fire warmed my back. I thanked my hostess for such a delicious meal, '*Kala shimbu shedra du, tujaychay.*'

The living room in which we both ate and lounged afterwards was large, with the ceiling supported on carved and painted wooden columns. Around the walls hung woollen tapestries, and against the walls stood cupboards and chests of brightly painted wood. The stone floor shone like glass and scattered around were colourful rugs depicting dragons, peacocks, flowers and extravagant insects.

In one corner was the house altar in front of which burned a butter lamp. The several idols, including a seated Buddha, wore diadems of pure gold and turquoise. In dishes at the feet of the idols were offerings of butter, fresh water, and dried grasses, their stems pushed into a bowl of multi-coloured grains of rice for support.

Butter lamps projecting from the walls on arm brackets illuminated the room in much the same way as our Western modern gas lighting.

By the end of the evening my back had recovered from the constant stoop and I spent a comfortable night on my first bed since I left Gangtok.

I awoke with the dawn on the following morning but on realizing I was in a place of safety, I felt profound solace and so turned over to resume sleeping.

Chapter 14

When I did rise I found that my first-floor room was on a back corner of the house and had two windows. One gave a view of the Chakpori University and two parks, called *lingkas* in Tibetan, and distinguishable by their groves of poplar and willow. The other window gave a view that extended across Wangdula's animal paddock and grazing on the bank of the Kyi River. Beyond lay the marsh and scrub where we had waited yesterday, and beyond the *chorten* was the Chinese mission with its many windows and curiously shaped tree.

I knew that Deng had been given the room next to mine. I went to knock on the door but it stood open and he was nowhere to be seen.

Proceeding downstairs I found that there was no one about. I stepped outside and found Wangdula and Bonjl in one of the barns sorting merchandise. I was amazed at the variety of curios and spices, jewellery and semi-precious gemstones, ivory-inlaid carved sandalwood boxes, censers and medicines which had been transported here by the yaks and dzos. But how much more might have been imported using the same number of beasts if wheeled carts had been used?

Bonjl presented me with my violin bow, which he said he'd found in amongst the merchandise. He offered no explanation as to how it could have got there.

Yongyu gave me boiled rice and dried fruits for my breakfast. I now had time on my hands to plan my course of action. I wanted to explore Lhasa but I had no intention of doing so as a painfully hunched peasant.

I could not travel through the thoroughfares as myself for fear of being arrested or being assassinated. As time went by it would become increasingly dangerous for Wangdula if I were to remain in his house, to say nothing of the tedium if I had to remain a virtual prisoner. I would then miss my seven per cent opium solution which I would certainly require to keep me sane. There had to be someone or something which could release me from the threat of the Men of Kham, the Chinese and Gyadze.

I returned to my bedroom and played a tune on my violin to inspire my dulled intellect. While playing I glanced out of the window at the Chakpori University and my intuition, coupled with common sense, told me that my answer lay there. There would be men of learning, intelligent men, to meet, and common ground upon which one might bond in friendship, in medical interests, just as there is at Bart's.

I heard sounds from below and so I laid my violin and bow back in their case and returned downstairs.

Langel was in the courtyard supervising Yongyu and the stockman. They were unloading the panniers carried by two donkeys, while another stood near by, waiting for the curious Tibetan wooden saddle to be removed.

Langel removed her upturned-bucket-shaped hat to reveal that her hair was now devoid of all ornament except for her plaits criss-crossing the crown of her head. She wore a leather coat with fur on the inside. Yongyu wore similar but plainer clothing and her hair was in a single plait. She was probably not much younger than Langel and perhaps not quite so buxom. She smiled readily, as most Tibetans do.

I made polite conversation and pleased both the ladies with my compliments. I also helped a little in unloading the donkeys, and found my way into the scullery to give the food to Yongyu to put away. It was a large room with a colourfully painted dresser opposite the stone and clay oven. In the centre was a wooden table with its top scrubbed white.

I next went to see Wangdula. He and Bonjl had completed arranging the goods he had brought from Sikkim. He pointed to a small group of goods set apart. 'Deng's,' he said. I noticed a child's top and whip amongst them.

It was time for me to show Wangdula my appreciation for all he had endured and done for me. I presented him with a bag of Indian rupees. I had no sangs, the Tibetan currency, to offer him.

By prior arrangement I remained in my bedroom when Langel's two children came to visit her. They were staying temporarily at Langel's sister's home so that they would not see me. It would be too much to expect them to keep the secret that there was a *philing* living in their house. No doubt they were excited with the adventure of staying with their aunt in Sho, and at seeing their daddy again after his trip, but they were another reason why I had somehow to obtain permission to remain in Lhasa. Ideally, I would like to be able to roam free to try to find out just what Gyadze was up to. And there was still my ambition of meeting with His Holiness the Dalai Lama to fulfil.

Over our evening meal of dried fish stew and vegetables we discussed my future. I asked about the possibility of my receiving help from someone at the Chakpori University. It came out in conversation that, every four years or so, boys were selected to attend schools in other countries. They returned when they were young men having learned another language and another culture, useful if such should ever be needed in future diplomacy or negotiations. Deng elected to make enquiries on the morrow in the hope of identifying such a man who had been educated in England. He agreed with me that such a man was either likely to be found actually at the Chakpori, or someone there would know of the whereabouts of such a man.

The following day was a miserable one for me. I was confined to the house, its courtyard and outbuildings. It is true that I did not have to rise early and that was some consolation. I did hear the early bustle in the courtyard as Wangdula loaded some pack animals with wares to sell at the market. Despite my dislike of rising early I would have dearly loved to join him; to have been able to become acquainted with the citizens of Lhasa and to have been able to explore its curious buildings and streets.

After I had breakfasted, I found myself in the company of Langel and Yongyu, but they were busy and so I occupied myself by reading through my journal notebook, now nearly full with my descriptions and adventures. I then went to find one of the ladies upon which to practise my Tibetan.

I found Yongyu in the scullery. I asked her the names of the vegetables she was about to prepare, with which she obliged me. Yongyu wore woollen clothing. The heat from the oven pervaded the scullery. Yongyu was in the middle of showing me how she removed seeds from one of the vegetables before chopping up the pod for cooking, when she waved her hand to indicate that she was hot. Without any ado, she removed her upper garment to reveal that she was naked from the waist upwards. She continued with her work and her explanations as though it was the most natural thing in the world to do; and I do believe that it was quite natural to her because Yongyu was quite naïve. Also I had once seen women so exposed working in the fields with men all around them. Then, I had been able to avert my eyes, but in such close proximity I found this a difficult thing to do.

I began to thank her almost immediately for improving my Tibetan, then beat a hasty retreat as soon as I was able without appearing to be discourteous. I had no sooner said, 'Kale, kale,' then I came upon Langel in the spacious living room.

I complimented Langel on how quiet her two children had been on their visit, and how well behaved they must be. Possibly they'd been told there was a visitor in the house and they were not to disturb him. I then went on to say how well she had disciplined them but could not recall exactly the Tibetan word for discipline. So, instead, I used the Tibetan word for horizon or limits of and hoped that it would make sense.

Langel hid her mouth behind her hand and tried to suppress her laughter but it bubbled out. She threw both of her hands in the air and ran to the scullery. After what seemed only seconds I heard both Langel and Yongyu laughing hysterically.

It was then that I realized with some concern that I had

probably strayed, quite innocently, on to terrain regarded as a feminine province.

I returned to my bedroom and played my violin for consolation. I felt homesick. I longed to immerse myself in the pages of *The Times*. I longed for my seven per cent solution but, even if it were available, I knew that I would be very foolish to succumb in my present circumstances.

Later in the day I heard a knock on my bedroom door and the sound of giggling fading along the corridor. When I looked out I found a tray with food and a teapot on it, salt and rancid butter, a small bunch of evergreen, and a piece of Tibetan sweetmeat. At least Langel had not taken offence at my gaffe. Thank goodness Tibetans were such good-natured people. I had made blunders as we made our journey from Sikkim to Lhasa but men together can enjoy a good laugh about them without undue embarrassment.

I subsequently made further gaffes mainly by not responding in accordance with Tibetan social mores.

What I did not realize at the time was the affectionate significance of the bunch of evergreen and the sweetmeat offered me by Langel.

That evening I had composed myself sufficiently to apologize for my gaffe of that morning. Amid the general merriment I noticed how Langel's eyes shone, and by personally serving me an extra portion of food, she showed that she bore me no rancour.

Deng had found out that a Doctor Tchrerchy at the Chakpori University had been educated in England. However, as he was now the abbot lama of the theological faculty, Deng had been unable to gain an audience with him. He promised to try again on the morrow.

Wangdula tactfully suggested that it would be wiser for me not to play my violin as the distinctly foreign music that I played would sooner or later draw attention to my presence. This suggestion seemed to me to be infinitely more attractive than having my bow confiscated again.

I rose leisurely again next morning and looked out of a window to see the sunshine penetrating most of the Lhasa Valley. The steep cliffs above slopes came directly down to the valley floor. The Happy River, Kyi in Tibetan, sparkled at the edge of the meadow where Wangdula's beasts grazed contentedly. Wangdula's stockman was at work in the paddock; travellers were taking the opportunity to undertake essential journeys with enthusiasm, and all seemed to be right with the world. However, instinct and my memory of Gyadze's actions told me otherwise. The game was afoot and I had much to do.

Irrespective of whether Deng had been successful in obtaining an audience with Doctor Tchrerchy, I intended to meet him before the day had expired.

CHAPTER 15

I dressed, and breakfasted, and again regretted the absence of *The Times*. I had promised not to play my violin and I completed my journal of the previous day's happenings and then moped around.

I avoided going into the scullery.

I was engaged in thought and no doubt mesmerized by the flame on the butter lamp at the front of the house shrine, when Langel spoke softly to me. 'Is your God fierce or kind?' I had not heard her approach in her woollen shoes.

'Oh,' I replied, startled out of my reverie. In my basic Tibetan I said, 'He is kind but he has bestowed certain talents, gifts, on me, and therefore expects a lot of me.'

Langel frowned.

'Rather like a father expects much of his son.'

Langel gave an understanding 'Ah! You have a figure of him? An idol?'

I shook my head in the negative.

'A picture?'

'No. Not with me,' I replied, 'nothing like that.'

'Then how do you know him?'

I could think only of the crucifix as a symbol but could not hope to explain its significance. However, I tried to describe the cross and drew a sketch of it for her in my notebook. Langel seemed to understand.

The distant sounds of musical instruments filled the house: the sounds of horns, conches, drums, bells and cymbals. We looked through the window to see a colourful troupe proceeding along the Mani Lhakmang Road from the west towards the Jokhang Temple.

I became aware that Yongyu had joined us from the scullery but refrained from looking in her direction just in case she was not respectably dressed.

Following the band were Chinese men and women all dressed in brightly coloured clothing. Some of the men carried plates spinning on sticks, then came jugglers, and after them came young women weaving sinuous patterns in the air with long coloured ribbons on the ends of long sticks. More men and women came past gambolling, turning somer-saults in the air, cartwheeling and standing on on another's shoulders. These were followed by a girl performing acro-batics on the bare back of a horse. Lastly, came a man in a black cloak.

The troupe came to a halt near by where the road opened out a little. A crowd gathered around.

The instrumentalists changed their attention-attracting cacophony to a hauntingly beautiful melody, while different performers exhibited their skills, terminating with six men and girls balancing in a pyramid.

The man cloaked in black then came forward and produced paper flowers out of thin air and presented them to ladies amongst the bystanders. He next produced a fan from mid-air, rolled a piece of paper into a ball and spun it on the surface of the fan where it grew larger and took on the shape of an egg. He then took the egg and broke it to prove that it was, indeed, a real egg. For his pièce-de-résistance he held a square of cloth to show that there was nothing on either side of it. He held it in front of himself. A drum roll held us all in suspense, and then, with a clash of cymbals, he dropped the square of cloth to reveal a boy standing before him.

The instrumentalists then took up their discordant music and continued on their way towards the market place adjoining the Jokhang Temple.

Langel patted my arm. 'Look!'

I followed her gaze. She was looking at the roof of the Potala Palace high above the city of Lhasa.

A human figure was visible. I turned, but Langel was no longer beside me. Yongyu was staring as though mesmerized. I looked again at the figure. It was a lama or monk wearing a hat, the peculiar shape of which I had not seen before, and he was watching the troupe through a telescope.

Langel returned with Wangdula's telescope. She offered it to me. I studied the figure through it. It was wearing a yellow robe.

'His Holiness, The Dalai Lama,' Langel uttered hoarsely. 'My God-King.'

CHAPTER 16

D eng returned as dusk was gathering. He looked very pleased with himself.

'You've had a successful day?' I queried.

'A satisfying day,' he replied. He placed a bag into the palm of my hand. 'Take these. There are sangs enough to keep you in Lhasa a long time.'

The bag weighed heavy. 'You are the bearer of welcome news then? As well as proof that the value of ex-army tents is high in Lhasa?' I chided.

'Doctor Tchrerchy is proving to be inaccessible but—'

I held up my hand to interrupt him. 'I foresaw such an eventuality. We will proceed under the cover of darkness to call on him this very night.'

As dusk turned into night we ate our meal before setting off on the backs of donkeys in order not to draw attention to ourselves. I wore my tweed suit under my *tchomba* and my cowl to conceal my features. I did not pigment my hands and face as I wished to exploit the element of surprise on the monks at the Chakpori University who so assiduously protected the lama doctor.

I am not a card-player, but I am aware that there comes a

time when a game can be won or lost by the timing of when to produce the ace.

The dim illumination from the windows of the houses on either side of the highway helped us find our way. We travelled along the Mani Lhakmang Road through Sho and turned south into the Lingkor Road. We turned into the second road on our left and soon began the climb to the Chakpori.

I stopped short of the entrance at a suitable place and remained half-concealed in the darkness while Deng continued into the Chakpori. He took with him a sheet of Tibetan paper, thick and cardlike, upon which I had printed, in English, the Tibetan proverb which Deng had recommended, 'The highest art is the art of living an ordinary life in an extraordinary manner'.

Somehow, we had to attract Doctor Tchrerchy's instant interest, and this seemed to both Deng and me to be the best possibility.

It seemed a long time, waiting in the cold night air, before Deng accompanied by a group of monks came to find me. They escorted me into the university courtyard. As we entered the illumination of butter lamps, I dismounted and removed my cowl. At that the monks became very excited. As we entered the building, one monk blew a conch shell, and the vestibule filled with monks, all looking at their first white *philing*. I, in my turn, had never before seen so many shaven heads all in one place. I felt like a hen in a clutch of eggs.

I divested myself of my *tchomba* and saw faces grin and others grimace at my Western clothing. Some of the monks touched me, childlike in their curiosity. The atmosphere was pungent with the combined smell of butter-lamp smoke, incense and unwashed bodies.

We entered the Chakpori proper and proceeded along a corridor until we stopped outside a door. Someone knocked on it and a *chela* opened it from the inside. He gestured for me to enter. Deng smiled but held back. The door was closed behind me deadening the clamour which had attended my presence.

Seated behind a writing table of plain wood was a lama, probably in his middle fifties, clad in a brown robe, his head more balding than shaven. He closed a wooden-bound book before him and laid his writing brush aside. His eyes shone and he smiled to reveal uneven, stained teeth. He rose and took up a *khata* from the table.

He exchanged his *khata* with mine, saying, 'Welcome. It is good to meet you. I am Doctor Tchrerchy.' He indicated for me to be seated. His English was perfect.

I would have preferred Deng to have accompanied me but we had previously agreed that whenever appropriate he would hold back as if he were my *chela*, a servant, rather than my equal, which I regarded him to be.

'I am Sherlock Holmes.'

He raised the book which lay before him and took out from beneath it the Tibetan proverb I had sent him. 'And how do you live your life in an extraordinary manner, Mr Holmes?'

'I am a consultant detective. I solve mysteries, track down thieves and murderers.'

'You trace missing people? Missing objects?'

'Certainly,' I replied, 'but my *métier* is to solve baffling crimes. Such thefts, murders and mysteries as are often beyond Scotland Yard's abilities to solve.' I paused. 'However, that is not why I have come to Tibet. I earnestly desire to converse with His Holiness, the Dalai Lama. I come in humility and the spirit of peace and goodwill, and as one who desires to learn the meaning of life itself, and whether there is the continuance of life after death.'

Just then, the doctor's *chela* brought in tea. Both Doctor Tchrerchy and I withdrew our tea bowls, saucers and covers from within our clothing. Doctor Tchrerchy placed his tea bowl on to its saucer and the cover on to the bowl. Deng had advised me to retain either the lid or the saucer to signify my lower station. I replaced my lid in my jacket pocket and placed my tea bowl on to its saucer.

Just then I must have shivered. The air of the room was cold and heavy with the smell of incense that burned before the doctor's personal shrine. The butter lamps gave out little heat and only just enough light by which to read.

The *chela* poured tea from a teapot into his master's tea bowl, added butter and salt and replaced the cover. He then removed the saucer from beneath my tea bowl before filling the bowl and adding butter and salt. I was obviously regarded as of quite inferior social standing!

I fancy the doctor must have noticed me shiver because he said, 'Please forgive me. You feel the cold?' He turned to his *chela* and directed him to fetch juniper wood and to light a fire in the small grate.

He turned to me, 'We monks are trained to raise our body temperature in the cold. It is the reward for self-discipline resulting in the mind's control over the body.'

I made no comment.

The doctor frowned, 'You are Christian?'

'Yes.'

'Is it not unusual for you to seek out the spiritual leader of another religion?'

I explained what had happened at my parents' funeral, told him of Mycroft's words, and how Watson's words at the Reichenbach Falls had brought it all back to me. 'I have suffered considerable difficulty and experienced great physical danger in travelling to Lhasa and have been greatly incommoded in entering the Forbidden City,' I continued. 'All in the hope of meeting His Holiness.'

'In all honesty, I doubt whether you will meet His Holiness. He rarely speaks to anyone who is not of his council of advisers.'

The doctor watched me as I considered his statement. I, in turn, noted that curious slight fattening of his lower lip and the nicotine stain at the tip of his forefinger which, together with his discoloured teeth, denoted the habitual pipe-smoker.

The resin of the juniper wood exuded by the heat of the fire sizzled and flamed and fed even larger flames which briefly illuminated the whole of the room. Around the walls stood Tibetan books of handmade paper between carved wooden covers. The air was by now scented by the burning wood, overcoming the perfume of the incense.

I felt dejected. I had come all this distance … 'Then perhaps you would be kind enough to impart to me whatever knowledge you may have on such matters as the purpose of life and on the hereafter?' I waited.

'Perhaps,' he replied, 'perhaps.'

I had not travelled all this way to be frustrated this easily. I was determined to return to England a more enlightened man. 'I will not trouble you much more, Doctor Tchrerchy. I will be quite content with any scientific proof you may have of the existence of the human soul and of life after death.'

'Do you have any scientific evidence?' he countered, softly.

'Yes, I have,' I retorted. I then explained to him the experiment that Sir James Saunders and I had put into operation. 'Sir James is an ardent spiritualist, a man of the utmost integrity, and a very good friend of mine, who contacts the spirits of departed souls by means of seances. In order to disprove his experiences or to substantiate them, as the case may be, I had, at my own expense, had a death-bed constructed by an utterly reliable chemical balance specialist firm in Birmingham. As well as being a comfortable bed, it was a giant scales or balance, accurate to within one quarter of an ounce.'

The doctor frowned.

I knew that I had his attention. 'It is installed at Bart's.' I waited for the doctor's response. 'The hospital in London. I am sure you must have heard of it!'

'Ah, so,' he commented.

'Sir James has already nursed and attended hopeless cases using the bed. The terminally ill without friends or relatives are cared for on it. Often, too, tramps and destitute persons. These people are given every little comfort and delicacy possible during their last weeks and days. And then, when they are on the point of death, perhaps comatose, Sir James and, whenever possible, the hospital chaplain, joins the nurse in attendance. They release clamps on the bed which then converts it into a giant balance. Then they pray for the patient and for their soul to be united with God.'

Doctor Tchrerchy nodded his approval.

'At the point of death and for at least four hours afterwards, they take scientific notes as to the weight carried and to any inexplicable loss of weight. Such loss is subject to confirmation that it is not attributable to an emission of air, gases, solids or liquids escaping from the cadaver.' I looked the doctor in the eyes. 'Such loss of weight could then be attributable only to something else vacating the body – the human soul!'

The doctor moistened his lips. 'And have you and Sir James had any success, Mr Holmes?'

'On several occasions. With varying weight losses, the lightest being one and a half ounces, and the heaviest two and one quarter ounces.' I sat back with some self-satisfaction at the expression on Doctor Tchrerchy's countenance.

The doctor nodded his head. 'Seek and you shall find; knock and it shall be opened unto you.' He inclined his head sagely and smiled, 'Yes, I can offer you some scientific evidence of the existence and passing of the human soul. But first, tell me, do you go to such scientific lengths in pursuing your calling of consulting detective?'

The air was heady with the fragrance of the burning juniper and I felt somehow, 'safe'. 'Naturally. Crime detection is my passion and so I seek out the truth and the proof of it to my utmost ability. Why?' I asked. 'Do you have a crime for me to solve?'

'We do not suffer much crime in Tibet, Mr Holmes. Especially not in Lhasa.' He rubbed his chin reflectively.

'But a crime has been committed?' I could hardly contain my excitement. 'Please tell me about it.'

The doctor rapped his fingertips on the table top before him.

'You are uncertain of me,' I stated. 'Would you be able to think more clearly and be more decisive if you smoked your pipe?'

'Er. Probably,' said the doctor. And then realization came to him. 'But how do you know that I smoke a pipe? Someone told you?'

'Not at all. I noticed your nicotine-stained fingertip which you use to tamp down the tobacco, a slight thickening of your lower lip, signs like those. They would also have told me that you are right-handed if I had not seen you use that hand when drinking from your tea bowl!'

'Tell me about your most recent case, Mr Holmes.'

'My most recent case!' I exclaimed. 'Why, that one is not yet solved, but solve it I will.' I then explained about the throwing-star and my process of elimination of possible suspects by thumb-ridge prints leading me to be certain that it was one of the party of monks or one of the two lamas who had thrown it. I did not mention Gyadze by name.

'Would you show me your sketches?' he asked. 'I would like to see them.'

'They are at my lodgings.'

'Wangdula's house?'

'Yes. But how did you know?' I answered reluctantly, as I had been careful not to name any of my companions for fear of their becoming the focus of trouble for their part in assisting me to enter Tibet, and Lhasa itself, illegally. However, it seemed that the doctor enjoyed prior knowledge concerning me.

'Then,' said the doctor, rising abruptly, 'we have no time to lose.' He rang a small bell. His *chela* came in immediately and Doctor Tchrerchy rattled off orders to him in Tibetan so fast that I was unable to understand. He sat at his table and, using his brush and ink, the doctor quickly wrote in the curious Tibetan symbols, dried the ink in front of the fire, and folded and sealed the document with red sealing wax before handing it to his waiting *chela* with the instruction, '*Gyogo.*'

CHAPTER 17

‸

'We have had advance reports of your presence in Tibet, Mr Holmes. It was presumed that you had somehow made your way into Lhasa despite stringent measures having been taken in order to intercept you. At a council meeting this afternoon and at the instigation of one of the abbots, a warrant was approved and issued for the purpose of searching Wangdula's house in the expectation of apprehending you. It will undoubtedly be implemented just before dawn.'

'But this is dreadful news you give me!'

'Do not be alarmed, Mr Holmes. Now that I have met you I am even now having the warrant quashed. My *chela* will deliver that message to the Potala Palace. No further action will be taken. We have need of your services.'

Excitement at Doctor Tchrerchy's last statement over-whelmed my apprehension.

Just at that moment Deng entered the room.

'I want you to instruct your *chela* to return to Wangdula's now and to remove all of your belongings, and his, and to bring them here to the Chakpori University. He is to make sure that no trace of you or him can be found at Wangdula's, just in case there is a search.'

I smiled at Doctor Tchrerchy. 'Thank you.'

I turned to Nin Lee Deng, 'You heard that, Deng?' Deng responded with a nod.

Deng and I looked at each other with amusement in our eyes.

'Deng will be accompanied by a group of monks to assist him. He is to tell Wangdula only that he might get a visit from the Men of Kham just before dawn. He must not explain further. As there will be no trace of his guest no harm will come to him or to his family. He is to make no more than a nominal protest. He has children who might innocently let the yak out of the bag?'

I nodded in the affirmative.

'Then advise Wangdula to take them to a relative's for the night. You and your *chela* are welcome to stay at the Chakpori.'

Deng nodded his understanding and left the room.

Doctor Tchrerchy rang his bell and another *chela* or monk appeared. '*Poja or cha suma.*' He turned to me. 'You would like some more tea?' The good doctor then rattled off more instructions in Tibetan. 'I've ordered two rooms to be prepared for you and Deng.'

'Something has happened then?' I queried. 'Here? In Lhasa? And you want my help?'

'Can I trust you, Mr Holmes?'

I remember reassuring him that the matter, whatever it concerned, would be treated in the strictest confidence.

'I must then trust you, Mr Holmes. It is a matter of the utmost delicacy.'

'Please do not worry on that account. I will do nothing, say nothing, to embarrass you or the Tibetan authorities. Please feel free to confide in me.'

Just then, the *chela* brought in the tea. Doctor Tchrerchy asked me for my saucer, which then he instructed the *chela* to place beneath my tea bowl.

'This matter, Mr Holmes, concerns the highest station in the land. His Holiness. Two of his personal items have been stolen from the Potala Palace.'

'And they are?'

'A ceremonial *shamo* – a hat, and a ceremonial robe.'

'And what, pray, is their significance? When are they usually worn? Can you describe them to me?'

'They are both yellow, His Holiness the Dalai Lama's colour. His Holiness is the only person in the whole of Tibet allowed to wear the colour. His Holiness wears yellow at all times but only wears ceremonial robes when he is engaged outside the Potala Palace.'

'On what occasions does His Holiness wear them, please?'

'On three main occasions. The Great Festival, when he travels to and from the Jokhang Temple, when he travels to the Summer Palace, and when he returns.'

'On no other occasion?'

'Only impromptu.'

'Please explain.'

'His Holiness visits one of the public parks on occasion. He does it on the spur of the moment but even so, he does wear the ceremonial robe which has been stolen.'

'Pomp?'

'Exactly, Mr Holmes. For the purposes of pomp. However, he prefers to travel in an enclosed litter or sedan-chair direct into a walled garden in Jewel Park, his favourite, and so the public get only a fleeting glimpse of him at most.'

'The other three occasions ? His Holiness is on view to his subjects?'

Doctor Tchrerchy nodded assent. 'Without exception.'

'Then I am of the opinion that we should concentrate on those occasions. Does His Holiness have any other significant item of ceremonial apparel?'

The doctor frowned.

'Shoes, a sash, a special *gaou*, sword, anything?'

'No. Nothing else. Er, no.'

'You seem uncertain, Doctor Tchrerchy. I just wondered if the thief or thieves having stolen His Holiness's *shamo* and robe might possibly be planning to steal further items!'

'No. There is nothing else to steal.'

'The Dalai Lama does not wear a crown or carry any symbol of office?'

'Definitely not.'

A knock came at the door and the doctor's *chela* entered, threw more logs on the fire and replenished the butter lamp in front of the shrine. He then stood in front of Doctor Tchrerchy, made a slight bow and said, *'Dogo pa.'* He then left the room.

'Everything is in order. He delivered my cancellation of the warrant for your arrest.'

'Thank you, Doctor Tchrerchy. So the hat, the *shamo*, was stolen when?' I continued our conversation. 'Sometime today?'

'No. It was stolen some months ago.'

'And the robe?' I did know when the robe had been taken and the identity of the thief, but I did not intend to divulge that information at that early stage.

'The loss was discovered today.'

I knew that Gyadze was the thief, and that possibly he was responsible for both thefts, but to what purpose? The thread which caught on Deng's *kukri* scabbard could have come from no other garment than His Holiness the Dalai Lama's ceremonial robe. Whatever Gyadze's fiendish purpose, he was prepared to kill me or have me killed, so it must be a particularly vile crime that he was planning.

I did think about confounding the doctor by showing him the yellow thread and explaining where it had come from, but I decided to keep my own counsel. As only the Dalai Lama could wear those garments in public, their theft made no sense at all. I needed to find out more about this curious crime.

On Deng's return, I showed Doctor Tchrerchy, over yet another bowl of tea, my sketches of the thumb-ridges. 'And that,' said he, pointing at the pencil sketch of the thumb-ridges with the scar running across, 'is the manner in which you might one day identify your would-be assassin?'

'You seem dubious, Doctor. However, I have personal reasons for believing that your thefts and my incident are somehow connected. I intend to find out what lies behind it all.'

Deng and I were shown our rooms, which were austerely furnished. I could not prevent myself from leaping about with excitement; a practice of mine at my Baker Street rooms and of which Mrs Hudson disapproved. The game was afoot!

CHAPTER 18

❧

The sounds of gongs and chanting had disturbed my sleep during the night. But during my waking periods an extraordinary explanation for the events that had taken place came to me. On the following morning I resumed my questioning of Doctor Tchrerchy. 'Does His Holiness, the Dalai Lama have an identical twin brother? Do you know of anyone who might be able to impersonate His Holiness?'

'No, no, no, Mr Holmes. Quite out of the question. Anyway, he is too well known to his Council for anyone to attempt to take his place!' He looked quite shocked at the implication.

However, I was not as certain as the good doctor. It seemed to me from what I'd been told that only the members of His Holiness's Council, his immediate family, and those of the permanent staff at the Potala Palace knew him well. The ordinary public saw him only a few times each year and would know nothing of his day-to-day character. If, for instance, the Council could be eliminated, and the Potala monks and *chelas* dispersed, there was every chance that a clever impersonator of similar appearance could replace him. To contemplate the implications for Tibet were that to happen sent a cold shiver down my spine.

'I really would like to help, Doctor Tchrerchy. This is indeed a puzzling business and I am sure that I can assist you in getting to the bottom of it.'

'You seem very certain, Mr Holmes.'

'I am.' I looked the doctor in the eyes. 'I would like to examine the room or rooms from which the hat and robe were taken, please.'

The good doctor looked as though a burden had been lifted from his shoulders as soon as I said that I could assist.

'I will arrange matters,' he said.

I'd been told that the hat and robe had been stolen from the Potala. When Doctor Tchrerchy escorted me to the Potala Palace I would find a way of speaking to the chief lama. It was, after all, why I had travelled to Tibet, to talk to His Holiness the Dalai Lama. The warrant for my arrest had been quashed, so there was certainly no reason why I should not receive permission to stay in Lhasa, at least until I had brought Gyadze to justice.

Thoughts of Gyadze bothered me. He was a definite danger to me; I would have to be very, very careful. It seemed that I had rid the planet of Professor Moriarty only to find another arch enemy! Possibly the opportunity might arise for me to convince Gyadze that I were no more than a bumbling English eccentric! The idea appealed to me. Clever men are often easily taken in by the simplest ruse. If only I could somehow persuade him of that I would be regarded as no more than a curiosity. I could then be free to continue my investigations into his motives and intentions.

The doctor had duties at the Potala and was away for most of the day. Although Deng was free to come and go as he pleased, I was constrained to keep to one part of the Chakpori, close to the room alloted to me. I took some exercise by walking up and down several corridors off which lay cells of which my room was one. The doors were open and the occupants were engaged in prayer, meditation, reading, writing or drawing on thick paper with ink applied with a brush.

I returned to my room to make notes in my journal. I had used up nearly all of the pages in my notebook despite cramping my writing into the tightest possible space, without, however, impairing legibility. My possessions had been delivered to the Chakpori as Doctor Tchrerchy had promised, so I took up my violin and scraped a few bars of a popular tune.

When I stretched my legs again I found that every cell on my route had been vacated.

Presently a monk brought me a meal of *tsampa* and I prevailed on him to bring me hot water to drink to relieve the indigestion that I knew would surely follow.

In the early evening, and over tea, Doctor Tchrerchy related to me the events of the day. I noted that he frowned when his *chela* whispered in his ear. He tut-tutted impatiently. 'Despite my attempted cancellation of the warrant for your arrest, it was still put into operation. Wangdula's house was searched at dawn. As Wangdula and his wife were not still in bed but had had their first rice, it must have been evident to the enforcement officers that they had been forewarned. At the debate of the Grand Council your possible motives for coming to Tibet were discussed. Mr Holmes, I took it upon myself to remind His Holiness and my fellow advisers that we Tibetans take it for granted that we can send four or five of our youths to one or other of the European countries to expand their education. Why should we not offer the same courtesy to a *philing* who has travelled in the opposite direction?'

'Thank you, Doctor Tchrerchy. Did anyone in particular, by any chance, reveal how my presence in Tibet was known?'

'One of the abbots brought it to the attention of the Grand Council.'

I could guess which one! I was quite certain too, that the monks and two lamas had come across us by design and not by chance.

'Mr Holmes, I then took the yak by the horns and told the assembly of your presence at the Chakpori, and of our conversations which were, in a manner of speaking, really examinations of your motives for travelling to Lhasa. I also told them of your calling as a detective. As a result of which the warrant for your arrest was immediately declared null and void.'

I sighed with relief. One of my objectives in risking coming to visit Doctor Tchrerchy had been achieved.

'Even now,' continued the doctor, 'a document is being prepared which will bear the Great Seal of Tibet allowing you unrestricted passage to wherever you may wish to travel.'

My spirits lifted. This news was even better than I could have hoped for, and so soon. I was now glad that I had kept my counsel concerning Gyadze's involvement in the matter of the robe. I would eventually bring him to book.

'Furthermore, you are summoned to the Potala Palace to appear before the Grand Council tomorrow at noon. You should be formally invited to investigate the circumstances of the thefts of His Holiness's hat and robe, and you will be required to name the culprit or culprits if at all possible.'

I restrained my impulse to jump for joy but I could not prevent a smile of satisfaction from crossing my face. 'May I ask a favour of you, Doctor Tchrerchy, please?'

'Yes?'

'Would it be possible for me to return to Wangdula's tonight? I really owe him and his wife an apology for the upset of this morning.'

'Yes,' said the doctor, rather hurriedly I thought. 'I will arrange for you to have an escort while you are collecting your belongings.'

When I left Doctor Tchrerchy's room, a group of monks stood outside, rather in the manner of a deputation. I thought I recognized some who occupied cells in the Chakpori near my own.

As I walked away I heard the doctor explaining something, concluding with, '*Ya po re*'. 'All is well'. I knew enough Tibetan by then to make sure that I took my violin with me.

CHAPTER 19

U nder cover of darkness Deng and I, accompanied by about twenty monks, set out for Wangdula's house. Some of the monks carried staves. I was surprised when we turned south at the Lingkor Road, as I would have thought the shortest route was the way we had come, through the Sho district. The clicking of prayer wheels was all around me. I noted that some of the monks carried drums, cymbals and horns. Every monk not playing a musical instrument carried a butter lantern.

Deng and I rode on mules with all our possessions on another packmule. We were surrounded by the monks, who were all on foot. We all wore *tchombas* against the chilly air.

From time to time the monks chanted, quite melodiously, I thought.

I recognized the *chorten*, 'the seed of highest enlightenment', on the south side of the city where I had met Deng. The monks stopped there to say a prayer and for those with musical instruments to organize themselves.

'What's happening?' I leaned across to ask Deng.

'No time to explain. I'll tell you later.'

Then the monks played their instruments lustily, gaining

their second wind and increasing in volume as we passed the Chinese mission. They continued until we were alongside the marsh near to Wangdula's house, when the monks stopped playing. Deng explained to me, 'About six hundred years ago Tibetans send army to quell attacks from Chinese. They were so successful they reached gates of China's City where Emperor had Palace. They exacted tribute in gold and silks before they would agree to return to their homeland. The monks never miss opportunity to remind and irritate Chinese. The Chinese understand but continue to try to influence His Holiness the Dalai Lama and his Grand Council for Tibet to become part of China. Many benefits are promised but not freedom of choice and no autonomy within China. But Tibetans diplomatically advise Chinese that Tibet must remain completely independent.

'And blowing their own trumpets is the monks' idea of diplomacy, I presume?'

Deng ignored my remark.

'Mr Mycroft Holmes instructs his agents that Her Majesty's Government would like to establish embassy in Lhasa. So look out for any opportunity to persuade His Holiness's Grand Council. But in meantime they find other means to support Tibet in case of attempted invasion.'

I wondered if I now qualified as one of Mr Mycroft Holmes's agents! And I wondered just how many guns and how much ammunition Deng and his fellow agents had smuggled into Tibet. The pacifist Dalai Lama would certainly not be in favour of that happening if he knew about them!

'Given the feelings of the monks and the Tibetan populace towards the Chinese, I am surprised at the presence of

Chinese acrobats and performers in Lhasa. I would have thought that they were not welcome!'

'Gyadze responsible for them being here, Mr Holmes. They here on goodwill mission. Tibetan courtesy at least accepts them, but whole of Lhasa resentful of their presence because Gyadze responsible for inviting them. He not at all popular.'

'But surely that is what diplomacy is all about?'

'Perhaps so,' replied Deng, 'but Tibetans not like to be influenced by outside materialistic world. They prefer their own spirituality and superstitions.'

We came to Wangdula's house, where the monks left us unloading our packmule before handing it back to the monks. The monks continued their journey by the shorter route to the Chakpori University.

Deng and I put on our woollen shoes.

Langel welcomed us dressed in her turquoise and silver headdress and a blue-green dress decorated with silver beads. We exchanged *khatas* and were immediately served tea by Yongyu.

'You were expecting us!' I exclaimed.

'Doctor Tchrerchy sent his *chela* to advise us.' Langel frowned. 'How was it that he arrived here ahead of you?' She handed us a jar of crystallized ginger to help ourselves.

'I believe we travelled by the scenic route.'

Langel suddenly realized that we had come in the dark and made a little moue at me.

I went on to apologize for the inconvenience to which she'd been put, but Langel waved away my apology as being unnecessary. 'We enjoyed ourselves frustrating authority,' she said with more than a little self-satisfaction.

It was then that I recalled something my very good friend

Watson once said. 'You can always detect a couple falling in love when they start to playfully tease each other.' It pulled me up rather and made me wonder?

Yongyu served us a meal of casseroled pork with apple and just a hint of cinnamon, accompanied by wholesome piju – Tibetan beer.

On the following morning a group of monks called at Wangdula's house and presented their credentials for his inspection.

As usual, Deng had left the house before I rose. I was interested to see him accompanied by Tagstel bringing up the rear of the cortège.

Wangdula spoke at some length with the monk in charge, before I was given a horse to ride at the centre of the retinue, and then he took the horse's lead rein as we processed at walking pace towards the Potala Palace. We all wore *tchombas* to protect us from a chilly wind.

We proceeded along the Mani Lhakmang road towards Sho village, where three separate roads lead to different parts of the Potala. I was closely surrounded by monks and could only surmise that Deng had arranged these precautions against a further attempt to assassinate me.

I was surprised when we turned right at the crossroads to the east of the Potala. We passed a willow grove and then turned left towards the north side of the Potala Palace along the Chara Sampa road. The Potala loomed about fourteen storeys above us. We turned into the north entrance opposite the Snake Temple.

As we ascended the steep approach to the God-King's palace I pulled my Tibetan ear-flapped travelling cap more firmly into position as the wind whipped at my *tchomba*. I looked across the gilded serpentine decorations on the Snake Temple roof, which we had just passed and saw low grey and purple hills in the distance.

We rode two-thirds of the way up the hill before coming to the Saffron Gate guarded by monk police. I had hitherto only seen the Potala from its southern elevation, where its foundations started at the bottom of the hill, and it rose sheer above Sho village. I had the distinct impression that I was entering by way of the tradesmen's entrance. I dismounted.

I was escorted by the monk who had been in charge of the procession along a passage with windows overlooking the eastern part of Lhasa and with the Jokhang Temple the principal landmark.

We ascended a flight of steps and entered a large room painted in dismal ancient tans and browns.

A group of lamas sat in low seats in a semicircle, facing an empty throne-like chair. Their variously coloured robes and hats were a distinct improvement on the paintwork. Amongst the lamas was Doctor Tchrerchy. No one acknowledged my presence.

I was led to the back of the room, past windows overlooking the southern aspect of Lhasa spread far beneath. Kites were being flown from the park called Dodpal Lingka and all was framed by the Lhasa Valley in which the Holy City nestled.

I was directed to a seat a little distance from the Grand Council.

A *chela* struck a gong softly. After about two minutes curtains were pulled back revealing a doorway from which His Holiness the Dalai Lama emerged. He was wearing a loose yellow robe, and his distinctive yellow hat. The lamas rose as one and I rose with them. They all bowed and I bowed with them. His Holiness took his place on his high-backed throne. The *chela* who had struck the gong stood beside his master with a *khata* over his arm. At a signal from His Holiness the Dalai Lama we all sat again.

At a signal from His Holiness Doctor Tchrerchy rose and briefly outlined to the Grand Council the spiritual quest which had led me to Lhasa. Of how fate might have moti-vated me to seek enlightenment just in time to be of benefit to Tibet. That could be proved only by allowing me to put my scientific skills to the test. I should be invited to detect the thief or thieves and to retrieve His Holiness's robe and hat.

Many words were unfamiliar to me but I understood the gist of Doctor Tchrerchy's speech. He then spoke to me briefly in English to confirm what he had just said.

Amongst the lamas was one dressed in an embroidered robe who, I was quite certain, I recognized as the horseman who had been wearing the yellow robe beneath his *tchomba* – Gyadze.

Doctor Tchrerchy concluded with: 'You will now be intro-duced to the members of the Grand Council, and last of all, if he wishes it, to His Holiness.'

I will not bore you with the names of the lamas, but suffice it to say that as I approached each one and was formally introduced they all smiled in a friendly manner. I offered my *khata* which they took, and I accepted theirs in return. As I had only one *khata*, I exchanged the one I had received from the first lama with the *khata* offered by the second, and so on.

The only lama who did not smile, in fact he scowled, was Gyadze. He of the embroidered robe. When Doctor Tchrerchy introduced me to Lama Gyadze, Abbot of Tengyeling

Monastery, I found myself looking into intense, resentful eyes above a grim unsmiling mouth.

We exchanged *khatas*. I would dearly have liked to say something to the effect that this was our third meeting, but that would have put him on his guard. At last I had been introduced to all of the Grand Council members and now hoped to be introduced to His Holiness the Dalai Lama.

It would have been rude to stare at him, so I studied His Holiness from beneath half-closed eyelids. He was the man whom I had undergone privations and dangers to meet. He was a young man of about sixteen, no more than about five feet six inches tall, and of slim build. His hat made him appear regally tall. There was no welcome in his eyes but I thought I detected curiosity.

Doctor Tchrerchy stood beside me before his God-King, waiting for his approval to introduce me. I sensed that the Dalai Lama was about to ignore me, so I took the initiative. I bowed slightly to His Holiness and said, '*Gawn da*', Tibetan for 'Pardon me.' I turned to Doctor Tchrerchy and continued in my broken Tibetan, 'You have shown me such kindness, sir, may I exchange *khatas* with you to show the respect I have for you?'

A gasp went up from the members of the Grand Council at this egregious gaffe. I heard someone guffaw.

Doctor Tchrerchy hesitated and then exchanged *khatas* with me. Upon which, I said, 'Only now do I consider myself adequate to being introduced to your spiritual leader.'

I placed my *khata* across my wrists ready for acceptance, turned towards His Holiness and bowed my head so that our eyes would not meet, and offered my *khata*.

I was never so relieved as when I felt the *khata* being removed and another placed across my wrists.

Doctor Tchrerchy spoke. 'Omniscient One, I present to you Mr Sherlock Holmes of England.'

'Welcome to Tibet, Mr Holmes. Thank you for offering to assist.' Doctor Tchrerchy translated the Dalai Lama's reply.

The Dalai Lama took a scroll from his *chela*. He untied a yellow ribbon to reveal a document inscribed in Tibetan characters. His *chela* handed him ink and a brush. His Holiness inscribed it, presumably with my name, and signed it. His *chela* gently sifted sand on to it to dry the ink; he then applied a large yellow wax seal to it. The *chela* then handed it to me.

'You may travel where you will in Lhasa and Tibet but you must leave before the next season of snows. I'm sure you will respect our customs,' His Holiness said, with an amused smile. Doctor Tchrerchy translated. The Dalai Lama then retired through the curtained doorway through which he had entered.

The Grand Council trooped into an anteroom, and the doctor and I followed. A *chela* served us Tibetan tea and little cakes. I was relegated to my tea bowl only amongst such illustrious company.

'Is the Grand Council's work finished for today?' I enquired of Doctor Tchrerchy.

'Not yet. Astrological configurations do not bode well for Tibet. The State Oracle has been summoned to prophesy and he will be here soon.'

I made no comment but I was horrified to realize that these untrained men governed their country on principles of superstition. Then it was that I realized that my own country, and indeed the Empire, is governed by untrained men on principles of cynicism and supposition!

'At the same time he will be questioned about the missing hat and robe,' he added, 'and the significance of their theft.'

When we had finished our 'afternoon tea', Doctor Tchrerchy and I, preceded by a *chela*, mounted a flight of steps to a corridor pungent with incense. We passed His Holiness's private rooms. The door was open and I observed the simplicity with which it was furnished; I noticed particularly the Staffordshire pastille-burner before the God-King's private shrine. Seeing it gave me an instant pang of homesickness, but this was quickly supplanted by the challenge of the mystery in hand.

His Holiness's wardrobe was situated in a dressing-room on the south-west corner of the Potala Palace with a single window on the west side. His Holiness's hats, perhaps a dozen, were stored on shelves and covered with cloths for protection.

At a sign from Doctor Tchrerchy, the wardrobe *chela* removed a cloth and took a hat down from the shelf. He held it for me to see. I took care not to touch or handle it. It was delicately but ornately decorated. The size of it meant that it would have to be concealed in a basket or some quite large container to be smuggled out of the Potala. I dismissed any notion that the original would still be in the Potala, because I already knew that the robe with which it should be worn had been smuggled out beneath Gyadze's *tchomba*.

I examined the shelf with my lens but it was spotless, and so there was no clue to be found.

I turned my attention to the cupboard where the missing robe had been stored. I felt around the bottom of the cupboard in the dark interior. I scraped in the corners with my thumbnail and removed accumulated fibres and strands of yellow. The *chela* looked uncomfortable. I went across to the window with my findings and, using my lens, I compared them with the thread in my wallet. I felt certain that some of them could have come from similar robes to the one which Gyadze had worn, perhaps even the same one.

I felt uplifted as though I had just used my needle and a seven per cent solution. It was then that I noticed a ramp leading downwards below the window.

With Doctor Tchrerchy translating for me, I then questioned the wardrobe *chela*. 'So who has access to His Holiness's wardrobe?' I asked. The answer was: several of the Dalai Lama's personal *chelas* and, of course, the Dalai Lama himself.

'Who discovered that the hat was missing?' One of the other *chelas* had noticed the sagging cloth quite some time ago.

'And who discovered that the robe was missing?' The *chela* himself had found the cupboard door ajar and it was that which had alerted him to the fact that the ceremonial robe was missing.

'Who has access to His Holiness's private rooms?'

'Only His Holiness and his personal *chelas*.'

'What about the members of the Grand Council?'

'Certainly not!' was the indignant answer. 'Only His Holiness and his servants.'

'Is there any time when a member of the Grand Council might use the corridor leading to the Dalai Lama's wardrobe?'

'Only if invited. That happens from time to time when His Holiness wants to be accompanied to exercise either on the roof or in the gardens below.'

'Please show me the ramp.'

The *chela* led the short distance to a door at the western end of the corridor, some nine or ten yards from the door of the wardrobe room. I opened the door and looked out. The ramp was quite wide and I saw stains which I deduced were from horse droppings.

'Would there be occasions when a member of the Grand Council might leave by this exit?'

'Only with His Holiness.'

'Would it be possible for someone to enter by the ramp door and not be observed?'

'No. The door is kept secured from the inside.'

I smiled as though to reassure him. But my smile was really to put him off his guard. Gyadze must have had inside help and this *chela* was my prime suspect. 'Thank you.'

Doctor Tchrerchy and I returned to the wardrobe room. At my request the Doctor dismissed the *chela*.

As the *chela* walked along the passage I was sure that I heard him start to speak but his voice ceased abruptly, as though he'd been admonished into silence. I guessed the reason for that.

'Did you find any finger-ridge prints, Mr Holmes?' asked the doctor.

'I regret that I did not ,' I said quite loudly in English.

I heard the faintest sound from outside the room. I had intended to tell the doctor some heartening news but I held back. Instead, I said, 'Regrettably, Doctor, there are no clues and so I fear the culprit will never be found.'

The doctor hunched forward with disappointment and sighed. 'You have let me down, Mr Holmes. I had had the highest hopes of your talents.'

I shrugged. 'I'm sorry to have incommoded you.'

Just then that curmudgeon Gyadze entered the wardrobe room. I had been rightly prudent in withholding my findings. The lama beamed. 'What success can be reported to His Holiness and the Grand Council?' Of course, he had been listening in. He spoke his native language.

The doctor and I held our silence.

'Come, come. We have all been led to believe that Mr Holmes's powers of observation and deduction and analysis solve all crimes in the twinkling of an eye. Europe's most hardened criminals cringe at his very name.' These last words he spoke in English to add weight to his sarcasm.

I, for my part, grasped my opportunity, and averted my eyes in a suitably embarrassed, even foolish look, but my spirit rebelled. I could have cheerfully throttled Gyadze then and there.

'You had better return, Mr Holmes, to whatever hole you have been skulking in.' He turned to Doctor Tchrerchy. 'And I will save your face, Tchrerchy, by reporting to His Holiness and the Grand Council that he is no more than a harmless English eccentric.' He turned to me. 'Your talents, Mr Holmes, if you have any, I would suggest are more suited to Western society than to that of Tibet. Tchah!' He turned on his heel and left the room.

Doctor Tchrerchy raised his hand as if to stay his departure, no doubt appalled that Gyadze would damn me in his report to His Holiness and the Grand Council, and by so doing humiliate him, but Gyadze was gone.

I waited for his footsteps and those of his undoubted accomplice, the wardrobe *chela*, to fade away before peering around the doorway to ensure that they had, indeed, both gone.

I turned to the doctor. 'Allow me to revive your spirits, Doctor Tchrerchy. Instinct made me admit defeat when I should have been relating success. It would appear that my prudence was fortunate.'

'What do you mean?'

I continued: 'I have enough confidence now to to state that I know with certainty the identity of the thief who stole the robe, how he smuggled it out of the Potala, and where he took it. The same man no doubt took His Holiness's ceremonial hat.'

The doctor beamed. 'You can prove this thief's guilt?'

'Alas, I have no proof. Only circumstantial evidence. In any case I think that there is more crime in the offing. If we seek more information we shall eventually outwit our thief.'

The smile on the doctor's face faded. His eyes, hard and bright, held mine. 'The thief's identity, Mr Holmes. His name?'

'It is none other than Gyadze, and he rode his horse down that ramp while he wore His Holiness's robe.'

CHAPTER 20

❦

I accompanied Doctor Tchrerchy and his retinue to the Chakpori University. Deng and Tagstel brought up the rear.

The three of us dined in the communal dining hall. I completed the meal with drinking a tea bowl of hot water and so further compounded the rumour that I was eccentric.

I asked Deng and Tagstel to wait for me as I intended to return to Wangdula's. I thought the doctor looked relieved at that news.

We withdrew to the Doctor's private room where a juniper-log fire was burning. There, I explained about the thread from the Dalai Lama's robe, and showed him the fluff and threads from His Holiness's wardrobe. Using my lens, I pointed out the comparisons with the thread which had caught on Deng's *kukri* scabbard on the day we entered the Holy City.

'But what possible motive could Gyadze have for all this subterfuge?'

'I have my own theory,' I replied. 'I have dismissed mere kleptomania but not delusions of grandeur. The intention of his thieving must surely be for someone to impersonate His Holiness, but to what purpose is, as yet, unclear.'

'That is a ridiculous theory, Mr Holmes. You do not understand us Tibetans nor our customs. We all know where His Holiness is at all times. He spends the winter in the Potala Palace. He ventures into Jewel Park just occasionally. Always without prior notice. And always with a retinue of monks and lamas. In the spring, His Holiness presides at the great religious festival at the Jokhang Temple, and for the summer he travels to his summer palace in the cool hills just east of Lhasa.'

'And he returns when?'

'At the end of the summer.'

I summed up. 'His Holiness leaves the Potala on just two preordained journeys each year, and two or three other times to Jewel Park when the whim takes him!'

'That is so.'

'I think we have a three-pipe mystery on our hands, Doctor. Would you care to join me while I deliberate?' I offered him my tobacco pouch.

The hot resin in the logs hissed and flared, alerting my senses, for which I was grateful, as the cloying smell of the incense tended to dull my brain.

'What would happen if His Holiness was killed or died?'

'We would wait for two years, Mr Holmes, and then we would seek out his reincarnation.'

'You would not accept a replacement? A man who was perhaps the Dalai Lama's exact duplicate?'

'Under no circumstances whatsoever.'

'Tell me, Doctor Tchrerchy, who rules Tibet when you have a young Dalai Lama?'

'The Grand Council.'

'No particular person?'

'No.'

'Is there anyone who could exert undue influence?'

'Well,' Doctor Tchrerchy pulled at the lobe of his ear, 'his parents have great influence, of course, and inevitably a young child is bound to have a favourite or favourites amongst his elders, who could therefore influence him.' He puffed on his pipe. 'Mr Holmes, I think that you are pursuing the wrong line of enquiry.'

'Perhaps,' I conceded, 'but I am at present keeping an open mind. Doctor Tchrerchy, I noticed that Abbot Gyadze was the only lama of the Grand Council who wears an embroidered robe.'

'True. It is not disallowed but is regarded as distasteful.'

'But could it be construed as a sign of delusions of grandeur?'

The doctor shrugged.

We sat in silence until the thin curls of tobacco smoke finished. I then left the Chakpori with Deng and Tagstel and we returned to Wangdula's house.

I showed Wangdula and Langel my authority, signed by His Holiness, and bearing the Great Seal of Tibet, which allowed me unobstructed travel to any part of Lhasa and Tibet. They nodded their approval and wonder at it.

I rose on the following day and, dressed in my tweeds beneath my *tchomba*, I, accompanied by Deng and Wangdula, rode my horse along the Mani Lhakmang Road direct to the Jokhang Temple, the equivalent to one of our English cathedrals.

On the south side of the square in which it is set is the council hall, the administrative centre for Tibetan civil servants, and on the north side is the market. Tented and open stalls lend a rainbow of colour to complement the Great Temple. The stallholders compete with each other in the variety of foods and wares they have on offer.

I immediately attracted attention. Curious coolies and women wearing upturned bucket-like hats, and their children, gathered round me. I wandered with my retinue around the stalls, looking for Western-style notebooks or notepaper but without success. I purchased a pot of red ink. I could not face trying to keep my journal on thick Tibetan paper. I resolved to make myself a quill pen with one of Wangdula's goose feathers and write diagonally or at right angles across my pencilled notes.

Pilgrims were prostrating themselves on the paving outside the temple entrance. Then they moved forward in a swimming motion to prostrate themselves once again. No wonder the paving shone like glass! The three of us threaded our way between the pilgrims to beneath the overhang of the Jokhang Temple roof. A line of elaborately decorated cylinders, each with a handle, lay before us. On further inspection I decided that the decoration depicted gods and demons – both to be equally appeased, I supposed! I followed Wangdula's and Deng's examples by pushing the handles of each balanced cylinder around, until a sonorous bell inside struck, representing a prayer to the deities.

The smell of the butter lamps mingled with incense invaded my nostrils as we entered the temple. A monk robed in dark red eyed me with curiosity, but made no attempt to bar my way. My eyes quickly adjusted to the dimly lit interior. Meanwhile, the sonorous sound of the cylinder bells rang out prayers to the deities as pilgrims entered and left.

The temple was lofty. Not far inside was a lifelike golden effigy of some long dead saint. Wangdula and Deng assured me that it was the actual body preserved by freezing and drying and then covered in gold leaf.

There were others in sitting, reclining or in the lotus position. One appeared to be reading the Kangyur holy book held in one hand whilst resting the other hand on the Commentaries.

Monks, nuns and pilgrims droned prayers and chanted mantras, and all around me I heard the clack of revolving prayer wheels.

We stopped at a table littered with coins and semi-precious stones. Amongst the dark jasper, brown cornelians, beryls, jade, turquoise and chalcedony, sat lean yellow-coloured cats. Deng explained that they were trained to attack anyone unwise enough to attempt to steal any offering from the table, They stared unblinkingly. I was careful how and where I deposited a few sangs.

Huge wall banners called *thangkas* hung from ceiling to floor. Their woven scenes depicted religious pictures or geometric mandalas. Butter lamps burned in groups, just as candles are lit in Catholic cathedrals. I felt that there were several similarities between Catholicism and Buddhism in the obvious pious devotions of both.

I felt my whole being uplifted by the totally spiritual atmosphere.

We passed ranks of low stools arranged like English church pews until we came to the Dalai Lama's gilded throne. In a central position and on its own, stood a pedestal as tall as a man but empty.

'The Diamond Buddha is placed there when His

Holiness attends the great religious festival,' whispered Deng.

Questions immediately crowded my mind, but then was neither the time nor the place to voice them to Deng. But an idea began to take form in my mind.

We returned to the market where the women in their curious hats trimmed with fur and twisted coloured silks bargained with stall-holders.

An emaciated convict wearing a wide board around his neck, preventing him from feeding himself, pleaded to be fed. Shackles around his ankles hampered his movements. I gave a stall-holder sangs to the tune of two *karmas* to pay for food and drink to reimburse him for feeding the wretched fellow. I then understood the significance of Jesus's parable of the Good Samaritan.

'There is no burial ground attached to the Jokhang Temple?' I asked Wangdula.

Wangdula shook his head in the negative. 'The bodies of some saints are preserved as you've seen. The bodies of Dalai Lamas are preserved in the Potala Palace, but where and how is a closely guarded secret. Bodies of us ordinary Tibetans are handed over to the Dagteb.' He shrugged. 'They dispose of them as we disposed of the Chinese *tchapas* – by dismembering them and putting them out for the lammergeyers and vultures to consume.'

I then explored the centre of Lhasa and was not challenged by Men of Kham.

We ate a meal in a one of the inns near to the Jokhang Temple and watched men playing a game, not unlike the English Hit-a-Pin Bagatelle for small coins.

When I considered that I had seen enough Deng and

Wangdula accompanied me to the junction where the roads fork to lead to Jewel Park and the Chakpori University respectively. I left them to return to Wangdula's house while I went to see Doctor Tchrerchy.

CHAPTER 21

❧

As soon as I reached the Chakpori a monk took charge of my horse and led it to fodder and water.

I was immediately whisked into the university building and taken to Doctor Tchrerchy's room amidst the obligatory group of curious monks.

The doctor received me with an exchange of *khatas*, Tibetan tea was brought in and a fire swiftly lit. Pleasantries were exchanged, then we got down to business.

'Tell me, Doctor Tchrerchy, is it true that His Holiness has a diamond Buddha?'

'*The* Diamond Buddha, Mr Holmes. In fact His Holiness must be accompanied by it both when he travels to the great festival at the Jokhang and when he travels to his summer palace and back.'

'So that if someone intended to depose His Holiness, or to impersonate him, they would have to gain possession of the Diamond Buddha first?'

'No one can depose His Holiness the Dalai Lama, Mr Holmes. Even if he were to be imprisoned by the Chinese, say, he would still be our God-King. No one can take his place.'

'Except as his reincarnation?'

'Quite so.'

'But, say if the Diamond Buddha were to be stolen, and a person who looks exactly like His Holiness suddenly appeared? Could such a man, dressed in His Holiness's ceremonial robe and hat, depose the Dalai Lama?'

'Certainly not!' The Doctor looked shocked at my suggestion. 'His Holiness would have to be abducted without anyone's knowledge for that to be even remotely possible.'

'Without your knowledge?'

'Definitely.'

'But, Doctor, say if that were to happen and the Dalai Lama started to make pronouncements and issue edicts which were out of character?'

'Then probably members of the Grand Council would get together and several of them would be charged with questioning him covertly. I personally helped to question him and to pronounce him the reincarnation of the thirteenth Dalai Lama and so have known him closely since he was two years old.' The look on the Doctor's face told me that he was appalled by my suppositions. 'What you suggest is impossible, almost disgraceful!'

I pressed him. 'But what if the Diamond Buddha were to be stolen?'

'Quite impossible. It is kept in the Potala vaults under lock and key and is under constant guard. Please accept that it is impossible to steal. Quite unlike the stolen robe and hat.'

'And when it is being transported to and from the Potala, and the Jokhang, and the Summer Palace?'

'It is transported in a bolted-down cage and is guarded by twenty monks armed with staves.'

'And in the Jokhang Temple? With a capacity congregation?'

The doctor gasped. 'Steal the Diamond Buddha in the Jokhang Temple! Impossible! In front of a congregation of two thousand devoted worshippers? If you jest, Mr Holmes, it is in the utmost bad taste!'

'Then extra care must be taken with its transporting to and from the Jokhang,' I replied, 'for I have a hunch that its theft must be Gyadze's next objective.'

Doctor Tchrerchy was not long in terminating our meeting and so I returned to Wangdula's house.

I revelled in the freedom His Holiness the Dalai Lama had given me to explore Lhasa. It was not long before I knew all four corners of the city. Wangdula's two children returned to their home and from time to time I found their company charming and agreeable. In consequence, I became more fluent in Tibetan and learned more of Tibetan customs.

Tibetans practise polygamy. This I learned one day when enquiring of Langel and Yongyu after Deng, who had been missing for several days, only to be met by earthy laughter. They understood my naïvety.

'He is in Sho at his cousin's house,' said Langel.

'Oh!' I exclaimed in that mixture of politeness and latent curiosity which does not allow the question to be asked but at the same time implies the desire for further information.

'Deng shares his cousin's wife.'

'Oh,' I said, somewhat deflated and not a little embarrassed.

'Didn't you know?'

'Well, no,' I replied.

Langel dropped her gaze from mine. 'Many men share wives in Tibet.' She raised her eyes and reclaimed my gaze. 'Don't you think that is a good custom, Mr Holmes?'

There Langel had me. I was motivated to say, 'Yes,' but felt that Langel had a hidden purpose in asking the question, and so I was evasive with my reply.

During my explorations of Lhasa I travelled the whole of the encircling Lingkor Road. At a junction of several roads about half a mile from the Potala is one which leads north to the Sera Monastery where 10,000 monks live. Another road took me to a group of shops selling clothes, shoes and boots, and general goods. Close by is a boxlike three-storey building with a plain façade. There seemed to me to be a Chinaman or two always either entering or leaving that building. On further enquiries I was told that it was rented by the Chinese ambassador to house overflow administrative staff connected with the Chinese mission.

One day I saw the magician leaving the building on foot. He was the one who had produced a small boy from seemingly nowhere, but had obviously had him concealed in a harness within his clothing and had revealed him under cover of his cloak. I had the impulse to casually follow the magician but he went no further than the mission. I waited just out of sight for want of nothing better to do. I was rewarded to see him leave the Mission on horseback accompanied by Poo Shih Foo, Gyadze's right-hand man.

Tibet was claimed by the Chinese as a province of China. The Tibetans vigorously resisted their claim. They kept a small, but, I was told, a reasonably well-equipped army at the mountain cols connecting the two countries. Why then, I asked myself, did the British Government consider it necessary to smuggle arms into Tibet? Obviously, the existence of the weapons was not known to the authorities, but were those weapons held in anticipation of some event? This must have been something that my own brother, Mycroft, knew about but what could it have been?

Because of the nature of the mountains, which were very high, and covered in snow and ice all year round, the ever present danger of avalanches, and the inaccessibility of militarily well-guarded cols, direct invasion of Tibet by Chinese forces was all but impossible. That left the Chinese with only one other option: to take Tibet by stealth. Gyadze was planning to replace His Holiness with an impostor, and was in cahoots with the Chinese ambassador.

It was evident that my brother, Mycroft, knew of, or suspected some such scheme. Deng and I were both in Tibet to protect it from being taken over by the Chinese. If they were allowed to be successful then northern India would soon be in danger of invasion from the Chinese. India! The jewel in the crown of the British Empire! It did not bear thinking about.

Having explored the Lingkor Road, I turned my attentions to the route leading from the Potala Palace to the Jokhang Temple. The distance was about a mile or so and was mainly along the Mani Lhakmang. This road took the traveller from the Jokhang, past Wangdula's house, and, eventually, across the Turquoise Bridge, giving a direct route out of Lhasa.

But then I had a thought, the route also led past the building housing the Chinese administrative staff overflow and, of course, housing the Chinese performers and acrobats.

If an attempt was to be made to steal the Diamond

Buddha along this route, then there was no more logical place than near that building. However, I was assured that every inch of the route would be occupied by pilgrims and citizens of Lhasa, all anxious to catch a glimpse of their God-King. They would obstruct all exits from the route and that building could be easily guarded or just as easily searched if necessary.

I went to the Chakpori and made my peace with Doctor Tchrerchy with many apologies for upsetting him, and many compliments on the architecture of the buildings of Lhasa. I mentioned that I had been unable to find any Western notepaper and how I was struggling to make a reliable quill pen in order eventually to write my journal crossways in red ink.

Doctor Tchrerchy came to my rescue with a penholder that he'd brought back with him when he had been schooled in England, and some of Mr Gillott's excellent steel nibs.

We discussed the prudence of setting extra guards in the vicinity of what Doctor Tchrerchy scathingly called 'The Barracks' when His Holiness travelled to the Jokhang Temple for the Great Festival. It was merely a precaution on my part because, at that stage, I was unable to work out how the Diamond Buddha might be stolen. The fact that it was removed from its protective cage and set on a pedestal in the Jokhang seemed to me to give the most likely opportunity for its theft. However, how could it possibly be taken in front of 2,000 pairs of watchful eyes? How could it be concealed quickly enough to be smuggled out of the temple? It was very baffling, but of one thing I was absolutely certain: it was imperative that Gyadze had to steal the Diamond Buddha, in order to complete His Holiness the Dalai Lama's regalia if he was to be usurped.

I determined to be at the ready to apprehend Gyadze when he attempted the theft.

CHAPTER 22

∽

I occupied my time to the best of my ability. When I licked my steel pen nib in preparation for continuing my journal crossways in red ink, I felt like a schoolboy once again. Oh, but how I missed *The Thunderer*! There can be no newspaper in the whole world to compare with *The Times*. I would have been glad to read any edition, no matter how old.

I have not often been in the proximity of children but found myself the centre of the attentions of Langel and Wangdula's son Jigme, and daughter Zangpo. They were full of fun. I am certain that they were every bit as alert as my Baker Street Irregulars who often prove capable of obtaining information unavailable to me.

My writing crossways in red ink in my journal was a complete success. By writing at right angles to my earlier pencilled notes all was legible.

Advent Sunday came. 'Stir-up Sunday', my mother called it when she and cook prepared the Christmas puddings. I thought of Christmas and suffered a pang of homesickness.

To ease my melancholia, I told Jigme and Zangpo about our British Christmas festivities. How Santa Claus, dressed up in red, visits children and leaves them small gifts. They roared with laughter at something so unbelievable. I found this ironic and in marked contrast to their serious discussions of how demons could climb on to roofs in their mischief-making, but would slip on the steep slippery tiles and be hurled away by the curved eaves.

Early in December, all of Lhasa celebrated the Feast of the Death of Tsongkapa, the great reformer of Tibetan Buddhism.

Every household burned countless butter lamps on the roof tops and families chanted prayers in his honour. For supper, dumplings were served to complete the celebration.

As Christmas approached, I related to Wangdula and Langel that in England we also celebrated a festival at that time of year. I asked if they would mind if I gave the children small gifts. It would be a small gesture of thanks for their hospitality. I purchased small gifts for Wangdula's family and for Yongyu and Deng. I approached Doctor Tchrerchy as to what I should wrap them in as I could find no suitable wrapping paper. He advised inexpensive material such as *khata* muslin.

On my travels around Lhasa I saw the Chinese jugglers and acrobats entertaining the citizens of Lhasa and obviously endeavouring to promote Chinese goodwill.

I gave out my gifts wrapped in muslin *khatas* on Christmas Day. Kites to Zangpo and Jigme, silver and turquoise earrings to Langel, a silver bangle to Yongyu, and silver *gaous* to Wangdula and Deng.

Someone said that anticipation is better than realization, but the looks on their faces exceeded all of my expectations.

I suspect that Zangpo and Jigme had told Wangdula and Langel about my funny old man dressed in red, and probably Deng alerted them to English customs at Christmas.

Langel gave me a gift in return wrapped in red silk. I carefully unwrapped it to find a crucifix made of wood and painted geometrically in the brightest of colours. This was accompanied by *'Tashi Delek!'* as her nearest seasonal greeting to our 'Merry Christmas'. Zangpo and Jigme excitedly escorted me at the double to my bedroom to see a sign they'd made for it. 'Uncle Deng says that's your name,' said Jigme. What could I say? I couldn't deflate their efforts by explaining, so I said, 'Yes.'

'Say your name then,' Jigme and Zangpo urged. 'Say what we've written.'

'Ess aitch,' I said.

'Essach,' they repeated.

Yongyu put on a splendid meal of goose and apple sauce and root vegetables, followed by dried fruits and almonds. I found beside my plate an invitation from Doctor Tchrerchy to visit him on the morrow.

I suppose it was a combination of thoughts of my childhood, of my parents, and of their deaths being my reason for coming to Tibet, but that night I had the most extraordinary dream or vision.

I found myself on the bank of a wide stream. The sun warmed my back. The stream had pebbles along its margin. The pebbles were bright and various in their colours. They continued beneath the waters of the stream, where they were soon lost to the eye by the hammered-metal effect of the glinting surface.

Looking to my left I saw, between the gnarled and twisted trunks of ancient trees, snow-capped distant hills. Mosses and lichens grew on exposed contorted roots. Springlike green leaves hung from every branch and twig.

My eyes roved from left to right along the rugged grandeur of the valley in which the stream flowed. A range of small waterfalls fell from fern-clad rocks in a feeder rivulet not far away.

As my gaze continued to my right there were green slopes dotted with shapes which seemed to alternate between sheep and people. Beyond the slopes were smoky distant hills.

Over all was a pale-blue sky speckled with tiny brilliant stars, as if I could see the effect of the night sky in daytime.

I turned to see what lay behind me. I shielded my eyes, expecting the sun to obscure my vision but the precaution was not necessary.

Dropping my hand I saw a city – but what a city! It seemed to me to stretch to a limitless horizon. It comprised well-ordered avenues and squares fringed with trees, shrubs, and pillars with swags of climbing plants in many hues of green, yellow, cream, red and silver-grey. Standing proud amongst the avenues and trees were buildings of every persuasion. Spires, domes and elegant towers stood between airy colonnades, silver lakes, leisure parks, and floral gardens. There were houses which were more mansions than humble dwellings. And yet all were harmonious with their neighbouring properties. All was well-ordered, peopled and peaceful.

The air was faintly sweetly perfumed and a delicious taste lingered in my mouth. A half-remembered taste but one which, even now, I cannot identify.

For a moment only, I fancied that I stood on the brink of knowing and of being a part of everything. An odd but wonderful feeling. Then, just as quickly, the fancy left me.

From the direction of the city a young couple walked hand in hand towards me. They were smiling and each held out their free hand in welcome.

Then came realization. I looked hard at their faces, younger there than I had ever known them in life.

'But,' I exclaimed, 'this cannot be!'

'It is,' they said in unison.

'But you are dead,' I said to my parents. 'You are a dream!'

'No,' they both said, kindly but firmly. 'You are the dream, we are reality.'

And then I woke with a start. I sat up in bed. I was wide awake. I felt elated. I lit my butter lamp with one of my precious vestas. The dream had been vivid. It was unlike any that I had experienced before. My parents were radiant, as though they exuded a corona around them. I quickly came to the positive conclusion that that was no dream but a vision.

I had difficulty in controlling my exhilaration and preventing myself from whooping and dancing around my bedroom. Instead, I breathed in deeply to calm myself, then I wrote my experience into my journal without delay. It must have been about four o'clock before I could drop off to sleep again.

CHAPTER 23

✏

I visited Doctor Tchrerchy on Boxing Day in response to his invitation. I was well protected from the cold in fur-lined boots and gloves, and my heavy *tchomba*. I had to dismount and walk my horse up the icy incline to the Chakpori.

The good doctor wished me the compliments of the season. He accepted my gift of tobacco.

In return, Doctor Tchrerchy gave me a hand-printed text on heavy Tibetan paper, gummed to a brightly painted wood panel. The text read, 'And I say unto you, Ask, and it shall be given you; seek, and ye shall find; knock, and the door shall be opened unto you.'

Before I could thank him, he held his hands up, palms towards me. 'I have yet another gift for you. An intangible gift. The gift of scientific experience. Come with me.'

The doctor led the way to a part of the university that I had not been to before. We entered a long room, perhaps forty feet long. On either side of the room fires blazed, so that it was very hot.

The far wall was painted black and before it stood a low dais. At the near end where we had entered was a strange device. At first I thought it might be a different type of prayer wheel. It had a handle protruding from the side and a screw mechanism which obviously rotated a central shaft to which the spindles of two wheels were attached. At the ends of the spindles, on the rims of the wheels, were roundels of what appeared to be delicately tinted glass, about eight or nine inches in diameter. The roundels alternated between pink, yellow and blue on the one wheel and green and amethyst on the other.

In a framework at the front of the wheels were two pairs of holes. The whole framework stood about eight feet high with the two pairs of holes at eye-level.

Doctor Tchrerchy rotated the handle and as he did so the two wheels spun in opposite directions. As they did so the glass panels passed across the eye-holes, for that is what indeed they were.

He rang a bell and four monks entered the room. They placed screens in front of the two fires so that the room was shielded from their glare. They then extinguished several butter lamps. There were no windows.

One of the monks proceeded to the dais where he stood with his back to us and a second monk came to the wheel and grasped the handle.

'Now, if you will look through those eye-pieces, Mr Holmes, while I look through the others,' directed Doctor Tchrerchy.

I stooped and placed my eyes firmly in position. I could see the dim shape of the monk standing on the dais.

The wheels of the machine began to rotate. The glass roundels passed across the field of view of the eye-pieces until all of the delicate colours merged into one. As they began to rotate faster I saw a halo form around the monk's head and around his exposed hands and feet.

Doctor Tchrerchy called out to the monk turning the wheel to hold that speed, and then to me he said, 'You see something, don't you?'

'Yes,' I cried out, 'he has a halo. He is a holy man. He is a saint!'

'Keep looking.' The doctor called out to the monk, who immediately dropped his robe. He stood naked with his back towards us.

The halo which I had seen around his head, hands and feet now surrounded his whole body.

'But that's astounding!' I yelled.

'Keep looking, Mr Holmes, as it winds down.'

The wheels slowed and, as they did so, the halo around the monk dimmed and disappeared.

The doctor called, '*Ya po re*.' The monk put his robe back on.

The doctor repeated the process twice more with the co-operation of the two other monks before dismissing them with, '*Ya po re*. We will return to my room where I will explain.'

Over Tibetan tea and sweetmeats he told me, 'Those monks are not particularly holy men. They are ordinary mortals like you and me. What you saw were their auras. We Tibetans believe that a soul inhabits our bodies. It is the part which will leave our bodies at death and which will live in the *bardo* state or return into another body if we choose to reincarnate. That is Buddhist belief. However, what you saw is a scientific fact revealed to you by a simple device for the refraction of light. Normal human sight is unable to see the human aura, but a gifted few can see it.'

'I thank you, Doctor,' I said, and proceeded to relate to him my dream of the previous night while it was still fresh in my mind. 'That aura or corona was around my parents in my dream. It seemed to emanate from both of them.'

'That, Mr Holmes, was no dream. You have been granted a vision. There are different levels of reality. A dream is a reality when you are dreaming it but is so very temporary that it is immediately forgotten in most cases. Life itself is a temporary reality which ends when the body dies. A vision is a stronger form of temporary reality, and a window into the eternal reality, which you will never forget. The state which mankind refers to as death is, in fact, the permanent eternal reality. His Holiness deliberately leaves that permanent eternal reality, every time his body dies, in order to reincarnate to be with his beloved Tibetans. He knows that one day his work on Earth will be done and then he can remain in the eternal reality.'

I would have liked to have discussed what I had seen further, but meal time approached and I wanted to avoid an invitation to dine on *tsampa*. There was more goose and apple sauce awaiting me at Wangdula's.

I made my '*Kale, kales*,' and returned to Yongyu's cooking.

CHAPTER 24

❧

Snow covered Lhasa for the major part of January eighteen ninety-two. Because everything had to be transported on the backs of pack animals or coolies, the main thoroughfares were kept scrupulously clear of snow, ice and manure. It was essential to do so in order to maintain supplies of food and fuel for the populace.

I had come to Tibet for spiritual enlightenment and had been amply rewarded. There is no such thing as death, but I decided that there is life before death which has to be lived responsibly.

Having decided beyond all reasonable doubt where would be the most logical place Gyadze would choose to steal the Diamond Buddha, I spent time in the Jokhang Temple studying the pedestal and its position upon which the jewel would rest and its proximity to places of possible concealment. I came to the only conclusion that if it were to be stolen, then it would need something like a conjuring trick to succeed.

I saw the Chinese entertainers in the market place performing beneath an awning opposite the Jokhang Temple. The magician again produced a small boy from mid-air, or so it seemed. I was by now quite certain that the boy must be concealed beneath the magician's loose clothing, his feet and hands in some sort of harness flat against his master's body. The boy would then release himself on a given signal, to drop behind the magician's black cloth, then suddenly to appear at the magician's behest.

I wondered if it was for his skills that the magician had been invited to Lhasa by Gyadze, rather than to entertain and try to spread goodwill amongst the Tibetans? Certainly the theft of the Diamond Buddha would require a most original conjuring trick to succeed. Although I hadn't seen the magician with Gyadze I had seen him ride off with Poo Shih Foo, Gyadze's right-hand man. For what purpose, I wondered?

I divided my time between visiting the Jokhang Temple and the Chakpori University where Doctor Tchrerchy and I discussed occult matters, theological differences, the qualities of various pipe tobaccos, and a wide range of other subjects.

At every opportunity I further improved and widened my grasp of the Tibetan language.

Every day I looked forward to Yongyu's cooking.

Looking at my journal, I recall that it was on a crisp but sunny day in late January when I travelled to the Chakpori, only to find that the doctor was still at the Potala, but had sent word ahead, anticipating my visit, that I should remain, as he would like to speak to me.

It was late by the time he returned and I had already resigned myself to an overnight stay. As this had happened on several occasions already, it was a probability against which I was always prepared. I had become accustomed to travelling with my toiletries, notebook, pen and ink, crucifix and religious text.

After our vegetarian meal and *poja*, the doctor acquainted me with the business of the Grand Council which had kept him so late.

Apparently the monks of Tengyling Monastery had asked for His Holiness's permission to make a *thangka* to hang on a suitable building on the Lingkor Road for the occasion when His Holiness would use that road on his journey to the summer palace.

The Dalai Lama had expressed to Gyadze that he did not know whether to be flattered by the monks' request and grant it, or to be humble and refuse permission.

'Gyadze has a silver tongue, Mr Holmes. He replied, "That His Holiness expressed his humility in all things, and it was the monks' wish that His Holiness would allow the *thangka* to be made and hung by exercising that humility." He went on to say that it might be construed as false pride if His Holiness the Dalai Lama were to refuse. There was much debate amongst the Grand Council. Gyadze is not at all popular. But His Holiness is a young man and could see no harm in it, and so the monks of Tengyeling Monastery have been granted permission.'

This was a very interesting piece of news. I remember placing my fingertips together as I endeavoured to fathom some ulterior motive for the request.

'But,' said the doctor, 'rumour has it that the monks have already started making such a *thangka*.'

'So that it is not unreasonable to conclude that they intended to hang it whether they received permission or not?'

'Exactly. There are two other things of interest.'

'And those are?'

'The building it will be hung from is the barracks. The *thangka* will be of a size that will cover the whole front of the barracks.'

'That will be huge,' I replied. 'Is that normal for a domestic building?'

'The barracks, as its name implies, was constructed to house Tibetan soldiers more than a century ago. That is why it has such a plain, almost ugly appearance. That is the reason given why it should be covered as His Holiness travels past.'

He noted that I was lost in thought. 'Ha! I thought that snippet of news might arouse your interest.'

'I have come to the conclusion,' I said, 'that Gyadze does not do anything without purpose. I will certainly give this little matter my due consideration.'

We then went on to discuss the human soul. Since it was obvious that I was unlikely to have the opportunity to discuss such matters with His Holiness and in any case, the Living Buddha was such a young and relatively inexperienced man, I felt that I should make my enquiries with the good doctor. I had already acquainted him with my intention to produce a modest treatise on the subject on my return to London.

'What about backing up your scientific observations with quotations from religious books?' asked the doctor.

'Which quotations do you have in mind, pray?'

'In the Qu-ran is the saying, "In the alternation of the night and day and what God has created in the heavens and the earth – surely these are signs for a God-fearing people!" '

I considered that, saying, 'What if the person addressed – reading the treatise – is an atheist or agnostic?'

'Ask him or her to consider all of man's achievements, the steam engine, the pyramids of Egypt, and so on. Then remind them that man is incapable of creating so common a thing as a blade of grass.' He looked me straight in the eye, 'So who, or what made you, me – your reader, Mr Holmes?'

'Mm. You have a point there.'

'To return to religious quotations. What about chapter twelve of *Ecclesiastes* in your own Bible?' Doctor Tchrerchy could see that I was ignorant of it and so he continued, 'Or ever the silver cord be loosed or the golden bowl be broken....'

I was bewildered.

'It speaks of the death of the body, Mr Holmes, and what happens when death takes place. We believe that a subtle silver cord connects the soul to the body during life, and that it becomes detached or is loosed on death so that the soul can escape imprisonment of the body and can go on, can progress.'

I had never heard a sermon or a Church of England vicar preach on this subject.

'And what, pray, is the golden bowl?'

'Why, Mr Holmes, it is the aura, the halo, you have seen it for yourself!'

'Just what are you trying to tell me? Your machine? You have seen?' I jumped to my feet in excitement. 'You have observed the moment of a person's death through the glass panes?'

The doctor nodded affirmation.

I confess that I spoke before I had thought out the implications of my words. 'Would it be possible? Is there any possibility...?'

'Perhaps. We shall see. You will understand the difficulties. In the meantime I suppose you must remain another Doubting Thomas,' he said wearily.

On the following day I awoke in my monk's cell. A low melodious chant came from the temple within the Chakpori. I suppose the sounds of cymbals or bells had woken me. I looked at the crucifix and text which I had hung on the wall beside my simple bed. They inspired me and I gave silent thanks for the knowledge gleaned in Tibet that life continued in the same form, but on another dimension, after death of the body. Part of my reason for coming had been fulfilled. I could only hope to find out the purpose of life itself. That was, if anybody knew.

I had just finished my toilet when Deng arrived. His eyes seemed very bright.

'You have news for me?' I enquired.

'Information. Inexplicable to me but it might mean something to you.'

I waited.

'I have been observing the Chinese entertainers. The magician and acrobats meet Gyadze from time to time.'

'Thank you,' I said. 'You confirm what I already suspected. I also have news for you. You obviously know that the entertainers are housed in the old barracks, but did you know that the monks of Tengyeling Monastery are making a *thangka* to cover the front of it completely?'

Deng looked puzzled but said nothing.

'It is intended to hang it for the day when the Dalai Lama travels along that way to his summer palace. What do you make of that?'

'Have to think about it. Um. But more news. There have been complaints from shopkeepers near to barracks.'

'What sort of complaints?'

'Mice.'

'Mice?'

'They claim they overrun with mice and blame enter-tainers for them.'

I shrugged. At first it seemed irrelevant.

'They breeding them. They have been seen. Cages and cages of them. Hundreds of mice.'

'Hm.' I pondered this information. 'Perhaps they have a performance which involves a lot of mice. I believe that conjurors use mice as well as rabbits and doves for their acts!'

'Well, if so, it is going to be spectacular act,' Deng retorted tartly.

'You may well be right, Deng, you may well be right.' An idea was beginning to form. 'I thank you for telling me. The mice could have real significance.'

Deng just scowled.

'I hesitate to ask,' I continued. 'There would be great danger?'

Deng's scowl turned to a look of interest.

I confided in him my theory concerning the thefts of the Dalai Lama's ceremonial robe and hat, and the need for Gyadze to steal the Diamond Buddha.

Deng shook his head in doubt. 'For such deception to work, Gyadze have to arrange for all members of Grand Council to be killed, and His Holiness's *chelas*.'

'Or,' I said, 'he might get away with killing the four prin-cipal advisers and banishing the *chelas* and the rest of the Council members to monasteries in remote parts of Tibet.'

'How could he do that?'

'If he could carry out the substitution successfully, then the impostor Dalai Lama would order the banishment immediately. Neither the Council members nor the *chelas* would have the opportunity to say anything to anyone of influence until it was too late. The Chinese army would see to that. There would be new advisers and there would be one original – Gyadze.' I looked Deng in the eye. 'The four senior Council members would be assassinated.' I paused. 'Doctor Tchrerchy would be one of those and I want to protect his life in particular.'

'What you want me to do?'

'You will recall that at the star-throwing incident there were two masked men? One of them was Gyadze, I am certain, but who was the second? Is he the intended impostor?'

Deng nodded his understanding.

'I suggest that he is most likely to be at the Chinese mission. Failing that, he will be at the Tengyeling Monastery. Can you try to confirm my theory without endangering your life?'

'Don't worry.' Deng brightened. 'I'll enlist Tagstel's help.'

CHAPTER 25

⌒

During early February the weather quickly grew warmer with lengthening daylight. As Lhasa is on a latitude equivalent to Cairo, albeit at a higher altitude, I suppose the swift change in the weather should not have been unexpected.

All of Lhasa celebrated the Tibetan New Year with greetings of '*Tashi Delek!*' Yongyu served auspicious dipper with the main meal where the whole family united. Langel's sister and her family were invited. It seemed to me to be just like Christmas.

Tibetans have many celebrations throughout the year but my mind was preoccupied by my anticipation of the theft of the Diamond Buddha during the Great Prayer Festival at the Jokhang Temple, now less than two weeks away.

As the day of the Great Festival approached, I became restless and irritable. I missed being able to read *The Times*, and I missed Watson, who seemed often to be the catalyst for my thoughts and theories. Fortunately, I did have my pipe.

I returned to Wangdula's house one day to retrieve my tobacco in its oilskin pouch, which I had forgotten. I found a very angry Wangdula clutching his telescope and I was just in time to see a red-eyed Langel run off.

'You shall not have it any more,' Wangdula yelled after her. 'Silly woman,' he muttered to me. 'She thinks she has seen His Holiness, the Living Buddha,' he spluttered, 'at a window of the Chinese mission – those barbarians!' He spat and walked off.

I could not believe my ears. I rushed up to my bedroom and looked out of the window which overlooked the Chinese mission.

Oh, if only I'd had a telescope! I was certain that Langel must have known what or whom she saw. Was it not she who had pointed out her God-King to me when he was on the roof of the Potala? I wondered whether whoever Langel saw was wearing the yellow ceremonial robe.

I waited at my window but no one came to the Chinese mission windows. The branches of that tree peculiar to Tibet shielded the lower windows. So it must have been an upper window from where the false Dalai Lama had looked out. I kept watch for half an hour and when it was evident that my vigil was in vain, I returned to my horse and set off for the district of Sho.

The wind was uncomfortably strong as I made my way to Deng's cousin's home. I positioned my *khata* to protect my face. When I arrived it was to learn from neighbours that Deng and his cousin's family had gone kite-flying at Jewel Park.

I proceeded there to find a large crowd either involved in kite-flying or gathered in social groups.

The park was aptly named Jewel Park with its geometrical flower beds of early hyacinths already in coloured bud and in beds shaped to resemble cut gemstones. At the centre of Jewel Park was a walled enclosure surrounded by an ornamental lake. Potala Palace guards stood at both ends of the bridge leading to the enclosure.

I then understood the reason for the social gathering. His Holiness the Dalai Lama was within the enclosure, probably studying his subjects from some covert position, the observer and the observed both enjoying their roles.

Deng was with his cousin, his wife and several children; one of the boys bore a remarkable resemblance to Deng. They were flying kites. Theirs, together with the many others, made a colourful display in the sky.

While they were disentangling kite strings I took Deng aside and explained what Langel had undoubtedly seen.

'Your theory appears correct, Mr Holmes. His Holiness here last two hours or more.'

I smacked my fist into the palm of my hand. 'If you were Watson, Deng, I would say that the game is definitely afoot!'

'I've been thinking, Mr Holmes. If impostor is mere puppet of Gyadze then he able to be manipulated. Gyadze could become virtual ruler of Tibet. He might even be capable of double-crossing his Chinese helpers!'

'If the impostor doesn't obey Gyadze if and when he can be installed as the substitute Dalai Lama, then he will lose his life, Deng. Gyadze would find it easier to have his own way if he had an infant or child reincarnation under his influence.'

Deng nodded his understanding. He removed his cap and the wind tousled his hair. He scratched his head.

I continued, 'Or, if the replacement Dalai Lama positively discouraged civil disobedience and the tendency of Tibetans to revolt against their new masters, Gyadze would continue in favour of the Chinese and would doubtless lead an opulent life.'

Deng spat with disgust.

'Tonight Tagstel and I will scale wall of Chinese mission. There is tree at rear to help us see inside. Don't worry, we find out all we can.'

I paled at the thought. 'That sounds highly dangerous.'

'It is only way. We have already tried to infiltrate Chinese mission by applying for menial employment, but to no avail.'

'I do not like it. It is too dangerous.'

'So is my *kukri*. I can decapitate a man with one blow. Where will you stay tonight?'

'At Wangdula's.'

'I'll report to you there at dawn.'

When I had first met Deng and observed the tattoo on his wrist I had surmised that he spoke Chinese as well as the several other languages I knew about. Once again my observation had led me to the correct conclusion.

I spent a little time watching the kite-flying until I became uncomfortably aware that I, in my turn, was being watched by the curious inhabitants of Lhasa, and so I returned to Wangdula's.

Once there, I chose an appropriate opportunity to speak to Langel. I placed my finger to my lips to imply secrecy. 'You did not imagine what you saw today, Langel.'

Langel's face expressed her despair and desperation. 'But you said that His Holiness spent this morning at the Norbu Lingka!'

'One day, Langel, I will explain all and prove to you that His Holiness could be in two places at once, and that you are right. In the meantime please keep the sighting of him secret.'

She looked at me with little short of wonder and admiration in her eyes. 'You mean it is magic? How can he be in two places at the same time?'

'It is true,' I said, 'but only a few of us know how it is done. It is essential that we keep it to ourselves for the time being.' I replaced my finger to my lips.

I was glad my grasp of Tibetan was by now fluent enough for me to hold a reasonably sensible conversation with Langel.

CHAPTER 26

'Wake up, Mr Holmes, wake up.'
I felt my shoulder being roughly shaken. I opened my eyes. Wangdula stood beside my bed. 'Deng is in a bad way. Come quickly.'

I rapidly pulled my trousers on and wrapped my *tchomba* about me. I followed Wangdula with his lantern to the stables.

Lying in the straw was Deng.

Wangdula's stockman was coaxing Deng to drink water from a ladle. Several wounds had been bound with strips of cloth to form bandages but Deng was still oozing blood.

'He won't let me move him into the house,' said Wangdula.

I knelt beside Deng. 'Deng. What happened? Let us get you inside.'

'No time. No time.' He was breathing in short bursts. 'Near to death.' Deng swallowed. I swallowed too. 'Tagstel and I went over mission wall.' He gasped. 'I managed to see meeting.'

The stockman moistened Deng's lips using the ladle.

'Gyadze there. And a devil: Dalai Lama's double.'

I took no pleasure in having been right because everything seemed to be turning in the direction of disaster.

'Two Chinese officials. They had sketch. The barracks.' Deng fought for breath. His face was ashen. 'I lip-read. "Kill all advisers." Attack Holiness through thang...' Deng coughed as his voice tailed off. He lost consciousness.

I took the ladle from the stockman and soaked a handful of straw which I then placed on Deng's forehead. His breathing became slower.

Wangdula ran to the house. By the time he returned Deng seemed to have stopped breathing. One last low breath gently left his lips like a sigh.

Wangdula had a book under his arm. He opened the carved wooden cover and began to read by the light of the lantern.

Langel and Yongyu came into the stable just then. They each wore their hair in a thick plait and had their *tchombas* pulled around them. They placed incense and sweetmeats in Deng's hands, and placed a *khata* over his face, which was by now turning to the colour of putty.

At the end of each prayer that Wangdula recited, the four of them chanted, 'May he be placed in the state of the perfect Buddhahood.' After the second verse I was able to control myself enough to join in.

After several more verses the others ceased their responses and were silent. So I recited The Lord's Prayer aloud and finished with, 'We commit Deng's soul to his Creator.' Wangdula read some more, and then pronounced the words in the *Bardo Thodol*: 'Let this Book be auspicious; Let virtue and goodness be perfected in every way.' He closed the Tibetan Book Of The Dead. We all remained silent for perhaps two minutes.

'We must expect visitors,' announced Wangdula. 'Deng's

kukri is missing and a Gurkha aways carries one. No one could have inflicted those wounds on Deng without his adversaries having suffered injuries or death.'

He turned to Yongyu, 'Fetch a *tchomba.*' Then to his stockman, 'Kill geese and drain the blood off. I shall need blood.'

Then to me, 'Help me to unsaddle Deng's horse and be careful not to get blood on your *tchomba.*'

We all set about our tasks. Wangdula and I washed the horse and rubbed him dry, and then placed a blanket over him. We removed the muffles from his hoofs. Wangdula had examined him for injuries. We cleaned the saddle and belly-band.

'We must remove the horse-blanket at day break. It would provoke unwelcome questions,' said Wangdula.

When the stockman returned we searched Deng's clothing, but there was nothing to identify him. The stockman then bound his hands and feet together before wrapping Deng's body in the *tchomba* Yongyu had brought out. The three of us placed Deng's body next to a dung heap and the stockman shovelled dung around and upon his body to conceal it.

Dawn broke and the stockman and I removed all traces of blood from the stable, the yard, and gateway while Wangdula sprinkled goose blood along the Mani Lhakmang so that the trail of Deng's blood appeared to lead past Wangdula's house and away from it.

I went to Deng's bedroom where I found a bag containing personal belongings, a few items of clothing, his rifle and ammunition, and a hand grenade. The latter I placed on top of a high cupboard with my own rifle and revolver. Wangdula concealed Deng's other belongings. I remember that I sat on my bed and put my face between my hands and asked myself, 'Just how could this tragedy have happened? And to Deng, of all good people.'

Jigme and Zangpo were fortunately unaware of the happenings of the night, and so when Men of Kham arrived with Chinese officials we all acted innocently.

The officer in charge questioned me. He knew who he was looking for. 'Have you seen this before?' He laid Deng's *kukri* before me.

'Most certainly. That *kukri* belongs to Nin Lee Deng. Where did you find it?'

'When did you last see Nin Lee Deng?' barked the officer.

'Yesterday. In the Norbu Lingka. Why? Where is he now?'

'You have not seen him since?'

'No,' I lied.

Meanwhile the Men of Kham who accompanied the officer made a rough search of the house, stables and barns.

'What are you looking for? Is Deng all right?'

Because I feared they might want to take me in for questioning, I unrolled the Dalai Lama's scroll granting me free and unmolested passage while in Lhasa and Tibet. The Men of Kham left without my learning anything from them. However, I breathed a sigh of relief.

Less than an hour after they had left, a monk rode on horseback into the courtyard. He handed me a thick piece of paper on which was written in English, 'Dear Mr Holmes, I would appreciate your assistance. Geluk Tchrerchy.'

I accompanied the monk to the Chakpori. The monk seemed very serious and remained silent throughout the whole journey.

When we arrived, I was served *poja* in what appeared to be an anteroom. Presently I was led to a door and the monk indicated that I should enter. I opened the door and stepped inside a wide room.

Propped against the wall opposite the door were five headless corpses. Each had a *khata* covering the neck and each naked body was trussed up with ropes. Beside each corpse squatted a monk speaking quietly to the dead body.

I made a step back at the sheer ghastliness of what I saw. I was unable to conceal my horrified feelings. My facial expression must have given me away.

'What do you know about these?' a voice barked at me in English. I whipped around. 'What is your part in all this?' It was Gyadze speaking.

I was dumbfounded.

'Speak man. Is this why you were sent to Tibet?'

'If you are addressing me, sir, then kindly exercise some respect in the presence of these horrific deaths.' I paused and glared. 'I was not sent to Tibet. I came of my own volition and for my own spiritual and scientific purposes and for no other reasons.'

Impulse urged me to use the politician's ploy at the hustings of asking a question in return. 'What have these deaths to do with me? What possible link could I have with them?'

I then noticed Doctor Tchrerchy standing in the background with two Chinese men. Their mandarin dress betrayed their status as officials.

'You are linked with a *kukri* found at the scene of the crime, and which you have already admitted belongs to a colleague of yours.'

'That is no link at all. I am not responsible for another's actions. Perhaps his *kukri* was stolen! Find the owner. Ask him, not me.'

'We intend to find him, Mr Holmes, make no mistake about that.'

'We?' I countered softly, 'Are you then connected with these two Chinese officials? What does a Tibetan abbot have in common with the Chinese? Are you in effect a servant of these Chinese officials?'

I looked at Doctor Tchrerchy and saw the grim look on his face. Gyadze did not miss the implications in my questions.

'The crime took place on Chinese premises. I am merely assisting our Chinese guests and you are under suspicion.'

'Then you are wasting your time.' I turned to Doctor Tchrerchy. 'Doctor,' I said firmly, 'Was it your idea to summon me in so cursory a manner? If so, then our friendship must end forthwith. I have made it my profession, indeed my life's work, to pursue the perpetrators of crime, especially murderers, and not to support those who commit murder.' I then turned to Gyadze, 'Are you seriously suggesting that I am a mass murderer?'

'You haven't it in you, Mr Holmes,' he snarled, 'but in my opinion you know well who has. For now, I have more important things to do.' He left the room followed by the two Chinese officials.

Doctor Tchrerchy beckoned for me to follow him to his room where we sat. Both of us, I'm sure, were in a state of minor shock. 'I'm sorry that you've been put through this,' he said.

'But what was its purpose?'

'Gyadze hoped that you would betray yourself at the

sight, and perhaps confess to having had some part in the carnage.'

'Doctor!' I expostulated. 'However, if I could help in solving the crime...?' I sat back, then, as Doctor Tchrerchy made no reply, I concluded: 'It would give me great satisfaction.' I decided that now was not the time to mention Deng's death. I kept my own counsel.

'I had better explain one or two things,' said the doctor.

'Please do,' I urged.

'First of all, the bodies were brought here by Chinese servants. No explanation of where they were found or of why their bodies had been stripped of clothing was forthcoming.'

'Please proceed,' I said.

'The unidentified bodies were examined by one of my medical colleagues. In his opinion all of them died from sword or knife wounds. Knife or *kukri*!' He paused. 'Skin colour suggests that four are Chinese and one Tibetan. Two of the Chinese were decapitated with a single blow. The other three received several blows to behead them.'

I made no comment. We understood each other.

'My colleague is of the opinion that two were probably decapitated in combat. The remaining three are more likely to have had their heads removed after they had been killed by body wounds, in order to render identification impossible.'

I remembered Deng's boast about beheading with one blow. 'And the bodies were tied up?'

'No. The monks tied the bodies up as soon as they were brought to the Chakpori. It is the custom when someone dies a violent death to prevent their soul returning to the body and taking revenge on the nearest person. Five monks are talking to the souls to urge them to go on beyond the *Bardo* or to seek another more suitable body in which to reincarnate. Naturally, those monks would fear for their own lives if the bodies were not tied up!'

'Naturally!' What else could I say in such circumstances?

'You will continue to help us?'

'Most certainly. You were thinking of what I said to Gyadze? I was not going to let him know what I intend to do. No doubt he has spies who will soon report to him! May I commence with the bodies, please?'

I followed the doctor back to the room where the bodies were.

As was my habit I had brought my notebook with me. I made a pretence of examining each corpse, but my object was to compare the right thumb-ridges of the Tibetan's body with the sketch in my notebook to confirm that they matched those of Tagstel.

I was sickened to confirm that they were indeed his. Two dear friends had been killed. I felt remorse at my responsibility. I also looked at the right thumb-ridges of the four Chinese bodies but the tell-tale scar was missing from all of them. My would-be assassin was still at large.

'As four of the victims are Chinese, they are all likely to have been killed in a place associated with the Chinese. Gyadze mentioned Chinese premises. Also, they all have smooth hands, Doctor Tchrerchy, indicating that they were employed in clerical or other light work. Therefore we would be prudent to commence our enquiries at the Chinese mission.'

I could see that the good doctor was endeavouring to follow my reasoning.

'If we can find nothing there of interest, then we will

investigate the barracks.' This is the reasoned logic I would have adopted if I had been faced with the problem as a consulting detective. However, on this occasion, I was possessed of the knowledge that Deng and Tagstel had fought for their lives at the Chinese mission and had unfortunately lost.

I did not favour the Doctor with the information that my two friends were dead. He in turn did not ask whether I knew the identity of any of the victims. Perhaps he guessed that I knew the Tibetan's!

Doctor Tchrerchy rode his horse with a monk holding a parasol over his head. I rode behind in accordance with my lower station in Tibetan mores.

When we arrived at the Chinese mission the gates were closed as usual. I examined the road for signs of blood but by the time of day that we arrived hoofs of animal traffic had obliterated any signs, if there had been any. While I was doing that, Doctor Tchrerchy was courteously enquiring whether we could have access to the mission building and grounds; he was firmly refused. Remaining mounted I continued my quest by examining the wall fronting the mission and using my lens until I found scratch-marks on the stonework. They indicated to me where Deng and Tagstel had climbed over. There was no sign of blood.

What puzzled me was why Deng had chosen that point of entry. I concluded that there must be cover on the other side which Deng knew about from one of his sources. Possibly he had noted the terrain when he had applied for employment?

I continued my examination to discover the point where Deng had returned, either with or without Tagstel. I worked my way to the rear of the mission, still on horseback, where the boundary wall was higher in relation to the external ground level. There I discovered an area where the lichen and mosses had been rubbed off, but still there was no blood. A thorough clean-up had been effected.

By now I had the distinct feeling that everything I did was being carefully observed. From an upper window of the mission, no doubt. So I then explored the scrubland between the mission and the boundary walls of other nearby buildings. I scratched my head as if baffled. But I did not miss the swath of flattened scrub which led to the *chorten*. Another clean-up to remove Deng's blood, no doubt. He and Tagstel had undoubtedly tethered their horses behind the chorten so that they would not be easily observed from the rear of the mission. I could not help but remember how Deng and I had lain low near this spot on our first day in Lhasa.

There was another faint trail leading towards the nearby roadway, but I didn't go and look as I knew that any traces of Deng's blood would have been long since removed. Instead, I scratched my head again as though I was puzzled, and made my way disconsolately back to Doctor Tchrerchy.

When I returned to the front of the Chinese mission I found him in conversation with Gyadze.

'What a coincidence finding you here, Mr Holmes!' said Gyadze. 'No. Please do not detail your reasoning as I have already had it explained by Lama Doctor Tchrerchy.'

I stroked my chin reflectively and decided to appear totally incompetent again. 'A coincidence indeed, Abbot Gyadze, that we should both be here. Please excuse us. I am not enjoying much success. I must look elsewhere. The barracks perhaps ...' I trailed off.

I turned to Doctor Tchrerchy. 'There is nothing to report

here, Doctor.' I saw Gyadze's chief monk Poo Shih Foo eying me antagonistically over his master's shoulder, as Gyadze enquired, 'You have finished here, then?'

'Yes, Abbot Gyadze. There are no clues to be found here.'

We spent the remainder of the morning visiting the barracks, where I made pretence of looking for non-existent clues before returning to the Chakpori. There, in private, I revealed to Doctor Tchrerchy my discoveries at the mission.

'As Gyadze was anxious as to whether I had found out anything, it seemed to me to be imperative that he should think that I had failed utterly. Something important happened last night, Doctor Tchrerchy, and when I have further information to impart I will let you know. What I can tell you is that two men climbed over the wall and into the mission grounds, but only one returned.'

'And the Chinese have not yet found him, Mr Holmes?'

'No,' I said sadly. 'I doubt they ever will.'

I think the good doctor interpreted my meaning correctly.

'What I do not understand,' I said, 'is, why the bodies were so unceremoniously dumped at the Chakpori!'

'That is because you do not understand the Oriental mind. It is a warning. Gyadze and the Chinese will now feel every justification for any action they may take in the future. Let us hope that is all that happens. The Chinese can be quite without mercy.'

'Something else must happen, Doctor. Something very important. Whether you believe it or not, His Holiness – and the whole of Tibet are in deadly peril.' I said that very quietly but not so quietly that the good Doctor should not hear.

Two days later, as there was a good breeze, I persuaded

Langel to allow me to take Jigme and Zangpo to the Norbu Lingka to fly their kites. Langel decided to accompany us. She wore the earrings that I had given her at Christmas.

Langel and I admired the jewel-shaped flower-beds while Jigme and Zangpo flew their kites. Deng's cousin was not there with his family, so I persuaded Langel to show me where he lived in Sho. We called on him and because Jigme and Zangpo were in earshot, I enquired whether Deng were there. Deng's cousin admitted that he had no knowledge of Deng's whereabouts. I looked him firmly in the eye. 'The last time I saw him he was about to go on a very long journey, his last journey, as he has been called away rather suddenly.'

Deng's cousin held my gaze. 'If I understand you correctly, it was inevitable,' he commented.

I was glad he understood. I handed him the bag of *sangs* which Deng had given me. 'For his son,' I said simply.

CHAPTER 27

❦

The day of the Great Festival arrived. Doctor Tchrerchy had reserved me a seat beside him in the Jokhang Temple. Before taking my seat I took up a position outside the massive temple so that I would be able to witness the procession and the Tibetan pomp. I turned my back on the dark-red, black-and-gold-banded temple with its ornate carved woodwork and masonry. My stature gave me the advantage over the smaller average Tibetan and so I was able to observe everything and everyone.

Bystanders, in their dark clothing relieved with geometric patterned woollen panels, bright *gaous* and curious hats in a variety of shapes, stood all around me.

The sounds of copper horns and trumpets heralded the arrival of the vanguard, made up of serving monks from the Potala Palace. At an interval behind them came monks carrying banners decorated with texts in Tibetan which I was unable to read. Next came a band of mounted musicians brightly garbed. After them followed an army of monks of the Tsedrung order, also on horseback and in order of rank. A powerful order but I never found out just why.

Then came a group of high dignitaries and senior

members of the God-King's household. I recognized the Dalai Lama's *chela* whom I now regarded as a traitor. Alongside them marched tall figures of the bodyguard – huge Men of Kham, two either side, their shoulders padded, and carrying long whips.

Next came a litter carried by twelve monks dressed in cherry red, and on the litter, within a substantial gilded cage was the Diamond Buddha. I estimated the idol to be between nine and ten inches high. It was in the lotus position and was composed of a frame of pure gold holding the diamond, some four inches or so square, set in the abdomen. The large diamond flashed and sparkled in the sunlight from a myriad of facets. I realized that it would be valuable in any other country of the world but knew it to be priceless in Tibet.

Up to now the crowd had contained their excitement in a seemly manner but the appearance of the Diamond Buddha evoked gasps of delight and reverence.

Then men and women alike took off their hats and I too took off my deerstalker. Bystanders became quiet and stood silent with folded hands. Men of Kham carrying staves and at intervals of about ten feet accompanied the palanquin of the Living Buddha. The palanquin gleamed like gold in the sunlight. As it drew nearer I saw that it was open-topped and lined with yellow silk. The weight of it was borne by thirty-six men dressed in green silk cloaks and wearing plate-shaped caps of crimson silk.

A *chela* sitting in the back of the palanquin was holding a large parasol made of iridescent peacock-tail feathers above the Dalai Lama's head as he sat in a recess, where his subjects could see him.

Immediately behind the palanquin rode the five cabinet

ministers, including Gyadze, Doctor Tchrerchy, Lama
Dringru Abbot of Sera, a monastery of ten thousand monks,
Lama Raingnou Abbot of the Jokhang Temple, and the Lama
Shrinzelo, Principal of the Tsedrung Order of monks. All
rode splendid horses with saddles adorned with gold-and-
silver filigree work. Behind them came the eight senior
counsellors who completed the Grand Council.

Following, were the noblemen of Tibet, amounting to no
more than twenty, and wearing little caps which just covered
their topknots and were fastened by a ribbon beneath the
chin.

I then followed the noblemen into the incense-laden air of
the Jokhang Temple, pushing the prayer wheels around as I
entered. A large number of Tibetans crowded around the
temple but were unable to be accommodated.

I knew that Wangdula and Langel intended to be present
but I did not see them anywhere. As my eyes searched for
them I noted Chinese entertainers scattered among the
congregation.

The Dalai Lama sat on his throne apart from the congregation and surrounded by noblemen, abbots, lamas, and
Men of Kham. The Diamond Buddha coruscated on its
pedestal in front of butter sculptures three to four feet high.
In front of the Diamond Buddha were seated musicians
with copper trumpets, conch shells, cymbals, drums and
bells. Gyadze and his chief monk were seated close to the
percussionists.

I am sure that Watson, with his pawky sense of humour,
would have said that they risked contracting ringing in their
ears!

I noted that the percussionist had two pairs of cymbals,

one copper and the other brass, and both stood in a little rack close to him.

Two of the cats guarding the high pile of gemstones and money on the offertory table squatted, and the third paced up and down behind them. The gold effigies and mummified figures looked on out of blind golden eyes. Smoke from the butter lamps turned the air blue beneath the high ceiling.

As I moved my head to look around me, light sparked off the gold and gemstones on the offertory table. White and grey strands of smoke from incense burners curled into the blue butter lamp smoke, striating it to look like chalcedony.

I sat on the right side of Doctor Tchrerchy and his *chela* sat on his left. I studied the butter effigies. There were several of demons, two of skulls, and one was a large figure of a seated Buddha. It was about four feet high with a round serene face and a symmetrically round stomach with a central navel.

The entrance prayer bells ceased their resonant striking. Abbot Raingou led the congregation in prayer. Then the musicians struck up and a sacred song was sung. The percussionist struck his copper cymbals which I idly noted were painted red on the concave side. The brass cymbals, on the other hand, seemed to have something pressed between them.

There was a movement in the congregation near to me and Doctor Tchrerchy thrust a multicoloured cord into my hand and indicated that I should pass the end of it on to the next person. He whispered to me, 'The Rainbow Cord. Symbolic. It binds us all together as one.' I nodded my understanding.

All this time I had retained my attention on the Diamond Buddha. Mantras were chanted until several rainbow cords had been passed around and were held by everyone in the congregation. The droning of the mantras dulled my senses. Then the cymbals were struck and a fresh song was begun.

Suddenly, there were screams throughout the Jokhang. Ladies near to me leaped about and fell over the nearest rainbow cord while shrieking. They were looking at the floor, stamping their feet and raising the hems of their skirts. Then I saw the reason: mice. I had just enough time to realize that these creatures must be the mice that Deng had told me the Chinese troupe had been breeding at the barracks. They had obviously released them simultaneously at a prearranged signal: probably the striking of the cymbals.

I leapt to my feet too, only to nearly fall over the rainbow cord. I felt the movement of a mouse as it ran up the inside of my trouser-leg. I involuntarily bent my knee and kicked out in an upward direction. The mouse was ejected into the congregation – no doubt adding further to the panic.

The sound of thunder flashes and Chinese crackers came from all directions and billowed out dense smoke.

My attention had been distracted from the Diamond Buddha and when I looked again in its direction it was hidden by smoke.

Panic intensified. I was pushed and fell over. I tried to rise but caught my foot in the rainbow cord and again I fell. Smoke made my eyes smart and set me coughing. I wrapped my *khata* around my mouth and nostrils.

The tightly packed congregation around me scrambled to free themselves of the rainbow cords and to vacate the Jokhang.

I put my hand on Doctor Tchrerchy's shoulder to reassure myself he was recovering from the shock we had all experienced. I indicated that he should wrap his *khata* around his face. I heard the sonorous clang of the prayer wheels as people left the Jokhang and, no doubt out of force of habit, pushed the cylinders around as they escaped.

I held my ground, my *khata* against my face.

Presently the smoke began to disperse. The Dalai Lama was almost hidden behind his noblemen and Men of Kham, who had gathered around to protect him. They all stood petrified and aghast at something. I looked in the same direction. The Diamond Buddha was no longer on its pedestal.

The musicians were not in their places but Gyadze and his henchmen had held their ground. For a moment Gyadze allowed his features to reveal his thoughts as I saw a hint of satisfaction brighten his eyes and curl the corners of his mouth.

Doctor Tchrerchy's *chela* crouched beside his master, talking to him. 'Please stay with him,' he pleaded, turning to me, 'while I try to find some water.'

Monks were trying to prevent people from leaving the Jokhang. A proportion of the congregation had evacuated the temple, but the entrance was too far away for a fugitive to have taken the Diamond Buddha, and to have left the Temple amid such a mêlée.

I looked at the butter figures, the demons, the skulls and the Buddha. They were the nearest objects. Then I looked at the relics of saints and long-dead monks and nuns. There must be some hiding place for the Diamond Buddha.

I thought of the Chinese conjuror. Perehaps it was on

someone's person even now, concealed within their clothing.

The rainbow cords and personal belongings lay scattered where worshippers had abandoned them.

I confided my opinion to Doctor Tchrerchy that the Diamond Buddha must still be within the Jokhang. 'Doctor Tchrerchy! Did you hear what I just said?' He was rocking, crooning like an imbecile. I realized that he was in a state of shock, but such a condition could all too easily deteriorate into a stroke or heart attack. I looked round for his *chela*, but without success. All I saw was Poo Shih Foo, making his way in our direction. I felt suddenly afraid.

'He needs air,' said Poo Shih Foo. 'I'll help you take him outside.'

I moved so that I came between him and the good doctor. I plunged my hand into my pocket and thrust my tea bowl into his right hand. 'Kusho,' I addressed him couteously, 'He needs water.'

Poo Shih Foo thrust my tea bowl back at me. 'No water.'

'Ah!' I replied, 'No matter, here comes the doctor's *chela* with water.'

I sensed mischief if Poo Shih Foo could approach closely enough to the doctor in his state of shock. The Chinese monk, accepting frustration of his intention, turned on his heel and returned to Gyadze.

I had an idea when I looked at my polished wooden tea bowl in the palm of my hand. I put my finger into the bowl and upturned it, clamping my thumb on to the base in an attempt to preserve Poo Shih Foo's thumb-ridge print, which would be near the rim.

I firmly believe that the doctor's very life had been in

danger. The doctor's *chela* administered water to his master but it was some time before we were able to lay the doctor on to a litter and return him to the Chakpori.

That night I stayed at the Chakpori, fearing that Doctor Tchrerchy might not recover. His *chela* and I tended him until the doctor fell into a deep sleep. Before I retired to my bed I dusted my tea bowl with a fine black dust which I obtained from the doctor's fireback in his study.

A thumb-ridge print emerged with that distinctive scar which I had first observed on the murderous throwing-star intended for my destruction.

Doctor Tchrerchy was weak next morning but lucid. 'You were correct, Mr Holmes. Your theory appears to be resolving into fact. We must not, cannot, fail again, or all will be lost. The impostor Dalai Lama will direct that Tibetans must no longer resist the Chinese.' He paused. 'The next generation will be educated by the Chinese to consider themselves to be part of the Chinese nation, and Gyadze will betray his religion in favour of wealth and power.'

'I'm so glad that we agree on that, Doctor Tchrerchy, but saddened that my theory appears to be coming true. If you will excuse me, I must go to the Jokhang, and try to find the place where the Diamond Buddha has been secreted.'

'Yes, yes. Go with my blessing.' He waved me away from his bedside.

I took the Doctor's *chela* aside and made him understand that his master was in danger of assassination and that, therefore, no one was to be allowed in to see him. 'Absolutely no one.' I insisted.

When I arrived at the Jokhang, monk police were keeping the laity from entering. I showed them my document with the Great Seal of the Dalai Lama and they reluctantly allowed me access. Once inside, I had to repeat the process to pass monks who were rotating the prayer cylinders.

I made my way to the pedestal where the Diamond Buddha had been. I again had to show my document to monks who were sweeping up, making good damage, and restoring butter lamps to their rightful places. The sonorous clangs of the prayer cylinders vibrated in the dusty air.

A lama stood beside the pedestal, praying. He counted the prayers on his rosary of 108 carved-skull beads.

I searched around the area for places of concealment. My searching irritated him and he glared at me. I ignored his annoyance and said, 'Doctor Tchrerchy asks whether the Diamond Buddha has been found?' The lama shook his head and went back to praying.

A monk was collecting personal belongings. Where the musicians had sat he stooped and picked up something, frowned, and put it down again. He wiped his fingers on his robe. I allowed him to move away before I approached the object he had discarded.

It was one of the brass cymbals. I picked it up, noting the greasy smears on its convex outside. I turned the concave side upwards to find that it was painted ochre and was coated in grease. I smelled it to confirm that the grease was, in fact, butter.

The centre of the cymbal protruded like a navel hernia. I nearly dropped it in my excitement. I looked around for the butter sculptures but they had been removed. The butter Buddha! I remembered that the effigy had been fashioned with a full rounded stomach and symmetrical indented navel. I was certain that the cymbal had been used in its moulding.

I disturbed the praying lama again. It did not help that I inadvertently addressed him as 'Kusho,' which is reserved for monks. I apologized and addressed him as, 'My lord,' which placated him a little. I eventually ascertained that the Buddha was made by the monks of Tengyeling Monastery. All of the butter sculptures had been returned to their respective monasteries, on the instructions of Lama Abbot Gyadze, to avoid their melting and collapsing. Gyadze had lost no time as they were removed last night. And, of course, the Diamond Buddha had been swiftly concealed in the stomach of the butter Buddha, and the damage made good with the extra butter held between the pair of cymbals. And the one I held had been expertly used to restore the sculpture.

I returned to the Chakpori carrying the cymbal carefully. I explained to Doctor Tchrerchy how, in my opinion, the Diamond Buddha, under cover of the smoke, had been thrust into the stomach of the butter effigy. There obviously had to be a cavity in the stomach, and with the Diamond Buddha thrust into it, a further layer of butter concealed between the pair of cymbals had been applied, the cymbal rotated, and 'Hey Presto', as a conjuror would ejaculate, the butter Buddha had been restored. I added that I suspected the Chinese conjuror had taken a leading role in devising the trick of concealment.

'All is coming true that you predicted, Mr Holmes.'

'I fear so, but it gives me little satisfaction, Doctor, to know that your God-King's life is in mortal danger.'

Just then the light caught a thumb-ridge print on the cymbal. I dusted it with a light coat of black from the chimney. Poo Shih Foo had done the deed. On the print was that all too familiar scar. No wonder the print on my tea bowl had been so clear – it had been made with a greasy thumb!

'Mr Holmes, we must prevent the unthinkable from happening.'

'Could we not send a search party to the Tengyeling Monastery? Arrest Poo Shih Foo and Gyadze?'

Doctor Tchrerchy shook his head, 'I fear that they would not find the Diamond Buddha, and then His Holiness, upon whose directions only could such a search be ordered, would suffer much embarrassment and loss of face.'

'It looks as though Gyadze now has what must surely be one of the most valuable diamonds in the whole world!' I commented.

'Its value in Tibet is not intrinsic but is highly symbolic, Mr Holmes. The many facets remind us that there are many religions in the world – many ways to God – many gleams of light. Men and women worship a facet of God within the constraints of their personal religion. We Buddhists try to worship the Whole God, to embrace all the facets, and the diamond is nothing more than that mystical representation.'

It was a statement of fact. The doctor spoke with humility, without rancour and without false pride.

CHAPTER 28

❧

The whole of Lhasa seethed with the news of the theft of the Diamond Buddha and the desecration of the Jokhang Temple. The Chinese were blamed. All foreigners in such a situation become the scapegoats. I had one or two uncomfortable moments. Overnight, several small businesses owned by Chinese traders were ransacked and set on fire. Men of Kham were posted around the barracks and the Chinese mission to prevent the same happening there.

To ease tension, the Dalai Lama and his Grand Council, abbots, lamas, monks and nuns reconsecrated the Jokhang Temple later that day.

At first I was alarmed by the possibility that the occasion would be used to substitute the Dalai Lama. I need not have worried. Had not Deng alerted me to when that attempt would take place? It had cost him his life to do so.

On this occasion the procession from the Potala to the Jokhang was accompanied by Men of Kham at intervals of only two paces. The golden cage, which would normally have contained the Diamond Buddha, was filled with crumpled yellow silk. The pedestal remained empty. However, the consecration took place without incident.

The Dalai Lama decreed that the next three days be dedicated to prayer and peaceful thoughts to calm the populace.

Rumours abounded in the following days, the most persistent being that the Dalai Lama would be magically reunited with the Diamond Buddha. I reasoned that Gyadze was preparing the ground for his impostor.

The State Oracle was called. On this occasion I was given the doubtful privilege of witnessing him in action. He was a youngish monk and I was led to understand that all state oracles tended to die young. He went into a trance, his face went puce and he seemed to have difficulty in breathing. He wore a breastplate and a huge thumb-ring which he used to beat a tattoo on his breastplate. He predicted danger for His Holiness, but that the Diamond Buddha would be recovered and a good outcome to the matter would result.

I rather felt that any seaside palmist in England could have done just as well in giving hopeful news, but without the ham acting!

Lhasa soon settled down back to an even tenor of peace and quiet. The Chinese entertainers were no longer seen on the thoroughfares; just as well, I thought, for their own safety.

Doctor Tchrerchy soon recovered and resumed his duties at the Chakpori and the Potala, but, while he had been absent, Gyadze had been able to gain the ear of His Holiness.

The thirteenth Dalai Lama is a mere boy, although old and wise beyond his years and even, perhaps, a little ingenuous. Gyadze however is probably close to forty years of age and is wily. He appears to have been educated in England and is much travelled. The Dalai Lama on the other hand is confined to the Potala, the Jokhang, the Summer Palace, and Jewel Park. Apparently he is enthralled by Gyadze's 'traveller's tales' and no doubt wishes that he could travel to strange lands and have similar amusing experiences.

While the Chief Councillor, Doctor Tchrerchy, had been confined to his bed, Gyadze had not been idle. As we sat in the doctor's study, he looked quite grim as he related to me Gyadze's latest infamy. The abbot had appealed to His Holiness's sense of duty as the spiritual leader of Tibetan Buddhists to form closer ties with the Chinese. Gyadze's reasoning was that by submitting himself to allegiance to the Emperor of China , the Dalai Lama would then, in exchange, become the spiritual leader of millions of Chinese Buddhists too; thus he appealed to the young God-King's vanity.

In the past, the four cabinet ministers had been irritated by Gyadze's attempts to influence His Holiness but on this occasion they were alarmed. The Tibetans prided themselves on having achieved the perfect society and would have to submit to change if they actually embraced Chinese rule and bent the knee to the Emperor of China.

Horror of horrors, the wheel would become the main means of transport throughout Tibet. 'I explained to His Holiness, Mr Holmes, that the sanctity of the symbol of Karmic cycle, rebirth, reincarnation and prayer wheels would be lost to Tibetan Buddhists forever.'

'And how did His Holiness respond, Doctor?'

'Favourably, I am satisfied to report, Mr Holmes.'

I summed up. 'Thus frustrating Gyadze's attempt to impose his influence on His Holiness. I suppose Gyadze thought that if the present Dalai Lama issued such an edict it would make his impostor that much easier to control. That, Doctor, was Gyadze's last attempt to influence His Holiness. His next attempt will be to substitute and kill him. I think the time has come when you must apprise His Holiness of the impending danger to his life!'

'You are so passionately certain of his impending peril.' Doctor Tchrerchy waved his hand to indicate that he had not finished. 'And I have no doubt that you are right. But how? Just how do you envisage the substitution taking place? His Holiness will be in his palanquin throughout the whole of the journey to the summer palace. You saw just how many men surrounded him on his two journeys to the Jokhang. Six-and-thirty bearers, guards alongside, and guards at both front and rear. Why, it would need a giant hawk to plummet from the very sky to pluck him away and deposit his substitute – and in full view of the masses! It cannot be done, Mr Holmes, it is an impossibility!'

At the doctor's description of a hawk plummeting, my mind raced; I saw it happen in my imagination. It could be done and I knew how.

'I know just how it will be attempted, Doctor Tchrerchy. It will not succeed I promise you that. But it is imperative that you make His Holiness fully aware that the attempt will take place and that he, His Holiness, will be at risk. An uncomfortable thought for anyone to know, but he must be told. I will devise a way to prevent the substitution taking place and for the impostor to disappear. We all have a part to play in beating Gyadze and his conjuror. But between now and that time there will be much to be done. Now, if I am right, this is my plan of action....'

CHAPTER 29

His Holiness was duly informed by Doctor Tchrerchy of the impending danger. I, in turn, was summoned to the Potala on the pretext of discussing when I would be expected to leave Tibet.

In reality, I discussed my ideas regarding the forthcoming procession to the summer palace. It was decided to restrict the knowledge of our intentions to the three other cabinet ministers. Gyadze must be kept in ignorance of our scheme at all costs.

And I wished that I could have confided in my dear friend Watson. By cunning questions, suggestions and ejaculations of wonder, he could give majesty to my simple art, which, after all, is merely the application of systematic common sense. When I have to relate my own story I have no such assistance.

However, I consider that I have incorporated sufficient clues in my narrative to give the reader an opportunity to imagine what might happen without giving the game away. It is for this purpose, and for this purpose only, that I will not spoil the reader's enjoyment.

I withhold details of the steps taken to foil Gyadze and I

omit discussions that took place. However, it was decided to take two more reliable and trustworthy people into our confidence – Wangdula and Trethong.

While certain modifications were being made to the Dalai Lama's palanquin in accordance with my suggestions, I spent more and more time at the Chakpori.

I missed Yongyu's cooking but I was becoming more used to eating and digesting *tsampa* and with less discomfort.

I also spent time in the Potala stables and workshops. I always arrived before dawn and left after nightfall. They were exacting days but rewarding because at long last I was able to anticipate Gyadze's scheming and oversee suitable counteracting preparations.

On the day that we completed our rehearsals in anticipation of what I considered would happen during the summer palace procession in a few days' time, instead of his expected, '*Kale, kale,*' Wangdula invited me to return with him for a late meal.

I was surprised when I arrived at Wangdula's to be exchanging *khatas* with Doctor Tchrerchy. No reason was offered for his presence nor did I consider it polite to enquire.

Langel was beautifully dressed, had silver and turquoise ornaments in her hair and she wore the silver earrings I'd given her at Christmas. Wangdula left us and when he returned he also was handsomely dressed in embroidered jerkin and trousers. Fortunately, Wangdula had given me enough time to put on my tweeds.

Yongyu served us a delicious meal of barley dumplings and vegetables. Doctor Tchrerchy's dinner was obviously totally vegetarian, but my dumplings contained morsels of fried liver and crisp pork. I suspected that Yongyu served both Langel and Wangdula the same.

After the meal, Yongyu cleared away the food vessels and left a dish of fruit on the table. She went out of the room. Then it was that Doctor Tchrerchy took over. 'Mr Holmes,' he said, 'I have been charged with acting as intermediary in making a serious proposition to you.'

I was taken by surprise. I looked at Wangdula and Langel dressed in their finery.

Wangdula nodded as if in approval of something. Langel shuffled a little in her black dress with pale and dark-blue panels and silver-beaded decoration. She studied her hands folded in her lap.

'As you probably know,' Doctor Tchrerchy continued, 'Tibetans practise polygamy and polyandry.'

My heart sank.

'I have been charged with expressing the proposition in English so that there will be no misunderstanding.' He paused. 'Langel proposes marriage. Wangdula approves her proposal and gives his blessing that you should join him in becoming Langel's second husband as his equal.'

I glanced at Langel and saw that she held her gaze demurely at her folded hands. When I turned my eyes to Wangdula his alert eyes crinkled at the corners signalling his approval.

'Langel would deem it a privilege to bear two children of yours, so that you will be on even terms with Wangdula.' Doctor Tchrerchy repeated that sentence in Tibetan.

Langel looked at me briefly, wide-eyed and intense.

I was aware of the honour being paid to me by Langel's proposal, but what was I to say?'

There was no gainsaying that Langel would have graced any assembly in Europe. Who could have imagined that so rare a blossom was to be found in the mysterious country of Tibet?

Women have seldom held attraction for me, for my brain has always governed my heart. There was one occasion when my eyes came to rest on the perfect clear-cut beauty of Irene Adler, but I had respect for her intellect when she outwitted me; I had no feelings for her. When speaking to Watson about her I always refer to her as 'the' woman. Having been in close contact with Langel over a period of time, I had grown to regard her with affection, as cousins often grow fond of each other, but nothing more.

At that point in my musings, Doctor Tchrerchy came to my rescue. 'Wangdula and Langel recognize that you are faced with a decision that will have far-reaching consequences, and that you may not be able to commit yourself immediately. But they both hope that it will not be long before you are able to say that you would like to share their home and way of life with them until death do you part.'

I wondered wildly and vaguely if that extended to allowing me to play my violin! I stammered my thanks and I feel sure that I used the word privilege in my reply that I would take up their offer to allow me time to ruminate on my decision.

I returned to the Chakpori with Doctor Tchrerchy. I discussed my plight with him conversing in English so that his *chela* would not understand. I explained that I did not love Langel. Not with the kind of love expected of a husband.

'Marry her,' was his reply. 'You will grow to love her.'

'But I fully intend to return to England and resume my self-ordained career as a consulting detective when my work in Tibet is completed.'

Chapter 30

I spent a restless night at the Chakpori. It was only after Doctor Tchrerchy and I had returned there that a confusion of emotions enveloped me. On one hand I wanted to explain my dilemma to the good doctor, on the other, I wished I had elected to occupy my bedroom at Wangdula's. After all it had 'Essach', as Jigme and Zangpo had called me, written on the door. It was as if I were already a part of their family. During the night I realized how troubled my conscience was regarding Langel.

I would rather have been seeking knowledge from Doctor Tchrerchy and had, indeed, been able to push thoughts of Langel to one side while immersed in abstract discussions with him. I had been deluding myself, however. As a gentleman, I was obliged to recognize certain duties.

Should I accept Langel's proposal of marriage and begin a new life in Tibet as second, but equal husband? Quite probably I should end up playing second fiddle to Langel once the novelty of having a *philing* for a husband had worn off. And what of any children? They would be half-caste. Life would, in all probability, be uncomfortable for them. Would I make a satisfactory husband? What would I do to earn my *sangs*?

Question after question ranged one after another through my mind.

I resolved to go to Langel on the morrow and somehow break it to her that it would be inappropriate for us to marry. It would assuredly cause us much pain, but it had to be done.

Next day I saddled my horse and headed for the Mani Lhakmang allowing my mount to take me there at its own pace. My reluctance increased in direct proportion to the distance I covered; I nearly did not complete my journey. When I did I dismounted with a heavy heart. The stockman took my horse and Yongyu welcomed me into the house. There, she served *poja*, and Tibetan sweetmeats. Langel joined me.

We sat on opposite sides of the low table on which the refreshments were set. I took my tea bowl from my pocket and placed it on the table. Langel looked me in the eyes, waiting. I placed my saucer beneath it. She still waited.

'I feel that I am not worthy to use the cover in your presence,' I said, in my halting Tibetan.

For answer, Langel removed the cover from her tea bowl.

Yongyu poured tea, added rancid butter, and then left the room.

'I fear that I have something to say which I shall find difficult.'

Langel waved her hand. 'Let it wait. Enjoy your repast.'

We ate and drank as my mind sought the best words, the right words.

Langel could not be nicer and it pained me to think that I must betray her affection.

Later, Langel made *poja*. She explained that she had sent Yongyu on an errand. I seemed to remember that Wangdula was out on business previously, neglected because of his involvement at the Potala Palace. If only he'd been there! I could have explained to him that, for every good reason, marriage would be out of the question as I must eventually return to London. I hoped to report a successful outcome to my visit to Tibet to my brother Mycroft.

It was not until I had returned to the Chakpori that I remembered the reason why I had gone to see Langel in the first place. As an honourable gentleman I should marry her. I would just have to find a way to resolve my predicament.

I later put my problem to Doctor Tchrerchy. He merely suggested that I could only undertake what I considered the correct course of action. If I did not marry Langel in this life then, he remarked, I would marry her in my next life, once I had reincarnated.

That set me to wondering whether our fellow men do reincarnate. Men such as Professor Moriarty, for example, were they given a fresh life, in which to help their fellow men and women and thus given the opportunity to atone for their previous evil life, thereby becoming worthy of a life with God in Eternal Happiness? I should like to think such is the case. Perhaps God would reject characters such as Moriarty instead recalling the souls of the humblest of men and women who had lived unremarkable but essentially decent lives. God had taken this latter course with my own parents of which I gained personal proof from my unforgettable vision.

I had previously taken the last of my belongings, my spare clothing and Deng's grenade, to the Chakpori on the last occasion that I had seen Langel. However, in two days' time I had a most ingenious crime to thwart. The successful outcome of this business would result in Tibetans retaining their own customs and values. Their contentment, their good natures and almost complete lack of crime, would be the envy of the world. I considered it my duty to foil a heinous crime and so, with good fortune, to preserve for Tibetans their happy way of life.

CHAPTER 31

꒐

The following day I again checked the enormous *thangka* which now hung from the barracks. I had noted the frame which had appeared overnight on the front parapet several days ago. I guessed its mechanism and was reassured that I was, indeed right, when the *thangka* was attached to it. It was cleverly put together in sections, but only the most observant person would be able to detect the places where flaps would open to release trained acrobats and the impostor Dalai Lama on the morrow.

Next day the whole of Lhasa took a day's holiday to witness the procession of their God-King from the Potala Palace to his summer palace.

Trethong, Wangdula and I arrived at the Potala well before daybreak. We all disappeared beneath the palanquin. I checked the spring mechanism on the trapdoor forming the well of the seat recess. The net to carry the body of the Dalai Lama's impersonator was firmly slung beneath the palanquin. Three leather bags accompanied it in readiness. All of this was concealed, together with Trethong and Wangdula, by a valance around the outside of the palanquin, made of weighted yellow material which touched the ground. It would drag on the thoroughfare when carried, to conceal what I had devised to happen there. The palanquin stood on support posts when it was stationary. It was imperative that no member the public could see under it at any time if our scheme was to succeed.

Trethong and Wangdula would have to bend their backs to walk beneath the palanquin. I couldn't remain with them. Someone had to be in the open, to be in the procession, ready to kill if necessary.

I coloured my arms, hands, calves and feet brown and donned my monk's robe which would form my disguise. All three of us would wear masks representing fantastic beasts from Tibetan mythology and which would completely cover our heads. Beneath my habit I wore my webbed holster and revolver. A specially made side-opening in my robe gave me ready access to the weapon.

As the component groups of the procession assembled we remained out of sight so that no one should know of our presence. Wangdula and Trethong kept reassuring each other, as well as me, that what we intended to do was the only course of action available to us.

The palanquin was raised and taken out of its quarters, then put back down in the Potala courtyard, in readiness. Except for another high-ranking lama, the Panchen Lama, leading the procession, it essentially took the same order as when the Dalai Lama travelled to the Jokhang Temple. It would leave by the Yellow Gate and proceed by way of the Lingkor Road and past the barracks on its way to the summer palace.

The army of monks of the Tsedrung order had formed outside the Yellow Gate. The band struck up noisily and the

Tsedrung monks fell in behind. I was glad when the band was out of earshot. There was a buzz of conversation all around the palanquin valance. We kept quiet and it was Trethong who heard that Gyadze was indisposed and was not, therefore, able to join in the procession.

'You were right, Mr Holmes, he does not want to be in the company of men he has arranged to be assassinated.'

Although the procession was essentially the same I had had to insist on necessary modifications. Monks from the Sera monastery of 10,000 joined the Men of Kham, all carried long staves and were to be spaced at seven paces. Their task was to make sure that no one made a run for it after Gyadze's plan had failed. My plan included the necessity to have Lhasa swarming with monks.

Two groups of experienced marksmen would walk to protect the Dalai Lama. One group would walk between the litter on which the Diamond Buddha was normally carried and the Dalai Lama's palanquin, and the other would immediately follow His Holiness. Wangdula had chosen only the very best from the experienced marksmen to whom he had been supplying arms. They were all dressed as monks and wore face masks of demons and deities. It would be their job to cleanse the barracks of any living person after the attempt had been made on His Holiness's life. This event had not been divulged to either His Holiness or Doctor Tchrerchy because neither would have approved of the killings. I would be amongst the group immediately in front of the palanquin, as I would need to be able to see the face of the impostor.

The cabinet ministers, though without Gyadze, would ride amongst the noblemen to keep them from being caught up in the action. With growing anticipation we heard the high dignitaries and senior members of the Potala household leave the courtyard. These were followed by the senior members of the Grand Council.

As the litter carrying the gold cage and its contents of crumpled yellow silk left the courtyard I steeled myself. I slipped my mask over my head, ducked beneath the valance, and joined the group of already masked marksmen.

As we left the Potala I was perhaps glad for the only time that Watson was not there to witness my antics. The marksmen, with revolvers and daggers concealed beneath their robes, had to act as monks and behave exactly as though they were in attendance. Regrettably, I think I attracted more attention from the crowds than the rest of my dancing companions put together, because I was the ungainliest.

The palanquin left immediately after us. As we proceeded I was deeply gratified by the sight of the enormous number of monks from the Sera Monastery. Lama Dringu, Abbot of Sera, had marshalled his monks to protect the members of the Grand Council by sheer force of numbers.

As we approached the barracks, I looked up at the huge *thangka*. It ran the full length of the barracks and was possibly some sixty feet deep. I observed the seams criss-crossing its surface and the secret that they concealed. I slowed my dancing in order to study the primitive beauty of the pictures on it which acted as an optical illusion to deflect attention from those seams. Each one represented a possible opening from which an assassin could drop and by means of which His Holiness could be spirited away.

Ahead of me were the members of the ruling Council of

Tibet. Immediately behind me was carried the courageous young God-King. I broke out in a cold sweat when I realized how close the moment was when their vulnerability would be put to the test.

I wondered whether Trethong, concealed beneath the palanquin, was leaving a trail of red betel-juice sputum in its wake.

As the great palanquin drew alongside the barracks, I danced, looking up at that framework holding the *thangka*. The crowd remained quiet, as was their custom, and with their heads bowed. They would see nothing until it would be too late to take any action to protect their God-King. His Holiness the Dalai Lama, his face pale, sat in the recess in the palanquin, waving a blessing over his subjects' heads.

I dared not blink as I trained my attention on the *thangka*. In doing so I saw a monk on the roof of the barracks. He was unmistakably Poo Shih Foo. He was holding a flag. Instinct told me that it was to be used as a signal, to instruct the assassins skulking in the crowds no doubt.

The framework leaned outwards from the barracks and the *thangka* jerked and dropped a few inches as though weight had been added to it. I immediately threw my mask off so that it no longer constricted my view. I snatched at my revolver. Poo Shih Foo stood at the curling corner of the roof above the *thangka*. I aimed at him and fired. He looked startled. This was the man who had attempted to assassinate me and, I am quite certain, would have killed Doctor Tchrerchy in the Jokhang if I'd let him approach the doctor. I aimed more carefully, using my left hand to steady my right hand and I fired again. Poo Shih Foo slowly twisted before dropping on to the eave with his arm hanging limply over it and releasing the flag, which dropped into the crowd below.

The percussion of my shots had paralysed the crowd and alerted the marksmen. Several of the Men of Kham ran towards me. One drew a short bow and an arrow from beneath his robe. I pointed towards the *thangka*. A cry of dismay rose from the crowd and there were screams. The Kham policeman halted, his face registering disbelief as the great *thangka* dropped over the God-King's palanquin.

It had fallen outwards from the barracks on the ends of ropes supported on booms which had been concealed by the framework and now swung outwards. The ends of the ropes pulled up the ridge of a tentlike roof, which was now covering the palanquin. Arms and legs of the many palanquin bearers protruded from the edge of the *thangka*. The palanquin remained upright on the supports concealed by the valance. Men of Kham ran at the tented structure, pulling at it futilely with their bare hands.

Just as suddenly as it had dropped, the *thangka* rose. Men of Kham and monks fell off it; two clinging for dear life were dislodged by blows from the back of the *thangka*.

As it rose, flaps dangled open from the *thangka*, revealing the seams which were, in fact, the access openings the existence of which I had correctly surmised. As the *thangka* lifted, so a figure crouching in the seat recess of the palanquin rose unsteadily to its feet. The figure was of a man dressed in the Dalai Lama's distinctive ceremonial robe, holding the Diamond Buddha in one hand and the Dalai Lama's distinctive ceremonial hat with the other. He pressed the hat firmly on to his head and raised the Diamond Buddha with both hands in a show of triumph.

I found myself looking at the youthful face of the Dalai Lama.

Breath left my lungs in a gasp. I had studied that face. It was – it must be- it had to be that of His Holiness, the thirteenth Dalai Lama. I hesitated. Something was not right. He did not give the prearranged signal. I was confused for a moment or so, as the joyful voices of his subjects rang in my ears. And then I knew what awful deed I had to perpetrate. He was not the real Dalai Lama and I had drawn the short straw. I had to kill him.

I aimed my revolver and fired so that the bullet passed several feet above his head. The impostor's face registered shock. He almost dropped the Diamond Buddha. Still he did not give the signal.

This time I aimed to shoot him between the eyes. I used my left hand to steady my right arm.

Before I could pull the trigger again, the impostor dropped through the trapdoor in the well of the palanquin. Men of Kham and monk police who should have been turning their attentions on me stood paralysed. I ran towards the bright palanquin.

As I approached, dodging between the guards, another figure rose up from the palanquin, in appearance exactly the same as the previous man.

Holding the Diamond Buddha aloft, he looked in my direction. '*Ya po re*, Holmes. *Guo-wa. Gyadze ce-gpyan.*' And the real Dalai Lama shook the Diamond Buddha as though it were some battle trophy. His face was flushed, in marked contrast to his earlier complexion which had been pallid with understandable fear.

At his cry of, 'It is well, Holmes. Blessings. Gyadze is a

jackal.' I flouted all Tibetan etiquette and convention and leapt on to the palanquin. I arrived behind the seat-well, where I stood behind His Holiness's back. The *chela* with his peacock-feather parasol had been knocked off the palanquin.

The Tibetan marksmen were climbing the *thangka*, just as the British sailors must have climbed the ropes and rigging of the French and Spanish ships during the famous Battle of Trafalgar.

I kept my eyes darting hither and thither. I was alert with revolver at the ready. Already I could hear sounds of gunshots from inside the barracks and muffled by the heavy *thangka*. I was all too aware that a man who covers another's back must be mindful of his own.

The Dalai Lama urged his monks and subjects to raise the palanquin and to bear it from that fearful place. At my direction the Men of Kham defended the barracks from being stormed by the common people and perhaps being set on fire.

I saw Trethong and Wangdula, with their masks hiding their identities, slip from beneath the yellow valance. Trethong carried the leather bag which held the decapitated head of the God-King impostor.

Standing back to back with the real God-King, I watched the reverence given to that brave young man. Activity could still be seen taking place at the barracks, until a bend in the Lingkor Road hid it from view. The procession continued its pedestrian way to the Summer Palace.

CHAPTER 32

❦

I remained at the summer palace until Lhasa had quietened down. His Holiness issued a proclamation declaring the next ten days to be days of peace, prayer and dumpling-eating.

Word was spread as swiftly as possible throughout the city and throughout the whole of Tibet as to what had officially happened. I found myself a hero and, at the same time, in danger of my life from the Chinese would-be assassins who had escaped in the crowds.

What was not divulged was what had happened to the impostor. He was said to have been spirited away to hell by evil demons. That, in my opinion, held a modicum of irony. Monks at the summer palace had retrieved the Dalai Lama's ceremonial robe and hat which had been placed in the second leather bag beneath the palanquin. After tying up the headless naked body in the third leather bag, and talking to the angry soul, they had released it to the Dagteb for them to dismember and put for the vultures to consume.

His Holiness was genuinely distressed when he heard what had really happened to his impostor. Doctor Tchrerchy and the other members of the ruling Grand Council had all been protected. Any assassins mingling with the crowds had no doubt become confused by lack of the flag signal from Poo Shih Foo until it was too late for them to act. By then the monks of Sera Monastery had closed protectively in large numbers around the Grand Council members.

Doctor Tchrerchy sadly brought me my belongings from the Chakpori. I was advised to stay at the summer palace until the Chinese assassins had been detected and arrested. I had been prevented from travelling to Wangdula's house because the Dalai Lama would not even countenance my risking assassination. In addition, reprisals could endanger the lives of Wangdula's family, and that I could not risk. I had to put on a good face in accepting His Holiness's hospitality.

Just how Langel and I were to meet in a safe enough place to get married I had, at that time, no idea. However, I did get news from time to time. I learned that Wangdula had been able to get Deng's body to the Dagteb. Also that Langel had a wonderful surprise for me when we were next able to meet. Looking at my gaily painted crucifix I tried to visualize just what it could be this time. I decided to send Langel a memento. I looked around my possessions but found no inspiration. I asked the advice of Doctor Tchrerchy on one of his visits. He made a choice, inspired no doubt by the summer palace *chelas*' reactions to my playing Handel's 'Silent Worship', by suggesting that I send Langel my violin. I reluctantly handed it over to him.

No reports were heard of the whereabouts of Gyadze. Rumour at the summer palace had it that he had been executed by the Chinese for his failure to bring Tibet under Chinese rule. The treachery of the monks of Tengyeling

Monastery had resulted in the monks of Sera Monastery instigating its dissolution. The lamasery was razed to the ground and the monks dispersed singly throughout monasteries spread all over Tibet.

I was at the point of wondering whether Langel had received my memento, when the Dalai Lama's *chela* showed it to me for my approval. It had been painted apple-green and decorated with a golden lion attacking a black and mandarin-orange dragon. Along the sides were painted ungainly dancers with angular arms and legs. One was wearing the mask that I wore on the day I foiled Gyadze, and the other had a good representation of my face! I was not impressed – I had grown rather fond of that violin – but I gave it back to the *chela* with my grudging approval.

One day, Doctor Tchrerchy and I sat down to talk sensibly about my future, if any, in my remaining in Tibet. 'I must stay,' I expostulated, 'I've all but promised to marry Langel.'

'If you do then you will put the lives of the family in peril. There are Chinese assassins out there still. It is no good, Mr Holmes, you must return to England for the sakes of all whom you love.'

Put so strongly, what else could I do but accept the painful inevitable departure from Tibet? His Holiness and I talked in Tibetan with the good Doctor helping to interpret difficult concepts. Young though he is, the Dalai Lama is wise beyond his years in spiritual matters. It was he who opined that every child in the world should be instructed in a religion and encouraged to respect it. At the same time there should be an exhortation to have respect for everybody else's religion. He went so far as to say that, in his opinion, world peace might be attained if every holy book of every religion contained an opening paragraph requiring the reader to show respect and tolerance to every person who came into their life, irrespective of his or her beliefs.

It was His Holiness himself who proposed the solution to my problem of escaping undetected from the summer palace.

Apparently in Tibet there was a Mohammedan holy artefact which had been taken in a battle over 1,000 years ago. The Dalai Lama had decreed that the holy relic should be returned to the Mohammedans and I would be disguised as a Man of Kham in the guard sent to protect its passage. It was reputed to be Mohammed's own sword which had been carried in battles when the early Mohammedans were converting nations to Islam 'by the sword'. If the provenance of Mohammed's sword was accompanied by ancient Tibetan documents, the artefact would indeed be deemed most holy by Mohammedans!

I asked whether I could be given, for preference, a monk escort to take me by way of northern Tibet out of harm's way and so return to England through northern India. This was granted. I was now known as 'Friend of Tibet', rather than as a *philing*, which I found rather flattering.

I travelled with a group of monks some thirty miles to the north of Lhasa. Each succeeding day was much the same, with the largest number of monks each lamasery could spare. In this way I went by way of Lhundup and Damshung to Nakchu, where I turned westwards towards Palgon. There I was given a bag of gold which roughly equalled the weight of Deng's hand grenade. Emphasis was put on the gift being for the purpose of helping me to pay my way when I left Tibet rather than a reward, which I would have assuredly refused, for I needed no money on this stage of my travels.

As the winter of eighteen ninety-two closed in I was unable to travel at all because of heavy snows. I enjoyed the Festival of Tsongkapa with its dumpling supper. A relief from the daily *tsampa* and heartburn!

When the snows thinned I recommenced my travels. Eighteen ninety-three found me in Wenbu, on my journey out of Tibet, where I was treated to dumplings and cries of 'Tashi Delek' to welcome in the Tibetan New Year. Soon after, my guides turned south and over a col and into India. There, I suffered melancholia. I had had to make the sacrifice of leaving Langel but it was necessary so as not to put her family's lives in danger. Also I thought of Doctor Tchrerchy; was it only last spring when he and I had been in Jewel Park? We were admiring the beds of hyacinths when he recited an Islamic proverb: 'If I had two loaves I would sell one and buy hyacinths. The one would feed my body and the other my soul.'

CHAPTER 33

❦

One late spring day six monks accompanied me into Himachal Pradesh. I could see no distinction between northern India and Tibet. It abounded with lamaseries. All the time I was making my escape from Tibet I had completely forgotten about Gyadze. At Ngaukla Monastery we were advised to be very careful because a band of four men had preceded us out of Tibet and were making enquiries, obviously about me.

At Ngaukla one of the Dalai Lama's *chelas* awaited my safe arrival. He handed me a letter from Doctor Tchrerchy written in English.

Dear Friend of Tibet,
Thank you for all that you have done for the Omniscient One. He asks of you one last favour. Would you please accompany the six Monks chosen to assist you out of Tibet to their ultimate destination of Khartoum? They are fluent in Arabic and have studied the Mohammedan Religion. The bearer of this letter also escorted the Mohammedan Holy Relic to the Ngaukla Monastery. Your escorting monks have been chosen to return it to the Khalifa.

I have such confidence that you will not decline that I thank you before the event.

You once asked me what is the meaning of life? I offer my own opinion. It is that there is only one God, The Creator, and God wants suitable companions. We are all manifestations of God. The human mind and body are such that God conceals Himself in us, as a part of us. We are free to do whatever we please. But this temporary reality, this life, is a period of development. Some men and women will develop into fit companions. The evil will be allowed to reincarnate or be forgotten by God. Most will choose to reincarnate – to have more than one chance to develop to the state of Buddhahood.

May God and His lesser Deities protect you.

Yours truly,

Geluk Tchrerchy

I expressed my consent to His Holiness's wish and my gratitude to the good doctor in my letter in reply.

The six monks and I decided to travel to Amritsar, sell our mounts, and from thence to travel by railway. Meanwhile, we remained on secondary tracks and descended from the Himalayas into the valley of the River Beas on the last stage of our journey to Amritsar.

We had travelled some twenty to thirty miles along the valley before we set up our tents. Behind us were fertile fields and in front the River Beas. On the opposite side lay a large settlement dominated by a Sikh Gurduwara temple with a finial-shaped gilded spire, red gold in the setting sun.

Four men on horseback drew to a halt on the opposite

bank. Something about their dress alerted me to them, possibly their lack of the turban so common around these parts. I pointed them out to my companions. 'I wonder whether that is the group we were told to beware of: the group of men who are making enquiries about me?'

We watched as they bartered the hire of a boat. They piled into it, pushing the boatman away, and leaving him stranded on the bank, yelling his annoyance. They were, no doubt, anxious about the onset of twilight which comes suddenly in this part of the world.

They rowed towards us. I went and armed myself because I knew my Buddhist companions had nothing more than hardwood staves with which to defend themselves.

The boat drew nearer. I exhorted my companions all to lie prostrate and to keep their heads well down.

I stepped into a ditch close to the bank. I called out in Tibetan, 'Who goes there?'

The reply came back in English, 'Why, if it isn't Mr Sherlock Holmes!'

I instantly dropped into the ditch and loosened the pin in the hand grenade that Deng had left behind.

Several bullets flew above my head. I lay on my stomach, took a furtive glance at the boat to judge position and distance, waited for the most opportune moment, and then lobbed the grenade. It rose in a parabola. I flattened myself deep into the ditch as several more bullets were fired in my direction and passed over me.

The flash lit up the sky. The explosion alarmed our horses which, fortunately, were hobbled, so they didn't get very far. Wildfowl concealed in the reedy bank created a commotion as they flew to safer places of hiding.

The firing ceased abruptly and fragments of wood fell about me.

I lay where I was, my revolver at the ready. Presently, I cautiously raised my head. The remains of the wrecked boat and four bodies, now some distance away, floated down the river.

CHAPTER 34

❦

At Amritsar I procured my first copy of *The Times* for two years. I wrote an article outlining Herr Sigerson's explorations in northern India and Tibet. I then went on to say that he would be coming to London early in eighteen ninety-four. In the meantime he was on his way to carry out a service for His Holiness The Dalai Lama of Tibet. I telegraphed it off to The Editor, *The Times*, London.

Briefly put, the monks and I travelled via Lahore to Sukkur, and then across Persia to Bandar Abbas, whence we embarked for Jiddah.

As soon as my companion monks had made known the importance of their mission they were treated by the Mohammedans to every courtesy. We re-embarked with an Arab escort to Port Sudan and thence to Khartoum where General 'Chinese' Gordon had been killed. As the Khalifa had moved to Omdurman some eight years previously, we were escorted on to a boat which took us across the Nile to the opposite bank to the new capital of Sudan. There, the casket containing Mohammed's sword, and covered in green silk, was ceremoniously presented to the Khalifa.

I had fulfilled my obligation to His Holiness the Dalai

Lama, and so I bade my companion monks *'Kale, kale,'* and set off for Montpellier where I have distant but discreet relatives. I telegraphed my brother, Mycroft, to advise him of my safe return and that Deng had been killed in action.

Mycroft telegraphed me by return to request that I write up my adventures in Tibet for Public Records. He also advised me that Colonel Moran was still involved in criminal activities. He suggested that I return to London in disguise, and find the proof to bring Moran to trial, on a charge of murder.

That would please me almost as much as my humble part in ensuring Tibetan independence.